After ten years of marriage, Nettie and Derrick are torn apart.

"Right now, more than ever, Derrick needs your support. Nettie, I promise you, you will be happy again."

Nettie drew herself up indignantly. "Don't make promises you can't keep, Lise. Derry didn't even have the decency to tell me where he is going."

"Trevor and I talked about that. In this area most men are sent to Camp Meade in Maryland. Do you want us to contact the Army for you?"

"No," she nearly shouted. "He must write to me first," she said stubbornly. "I'm not chasing after him."

"Did you argue before he left?"

"No. . .well, yes. I told him. . ." Nettie burst into tears; heart-wrenching sobs filled the quiet afternoon.

Elise rubbed Nettie's back the way she had often done when they were children and Nettie was upset. "You are with child, aren't you, dear sister?"

Nettie nodded and wept into her hands. When she looked up again her eyes were red and puffy. "What am I to do, Lise? Even learning I am having a baby didn't keep him home. And he is fully aware of what happened before."

SHIRLEY S. ROHDE, an author of many short stories and articles, makes her home in Pennsylvania. Shirley and her husband enjoy woodcrafting and being grandparents.

Books by Shirley S. Rohde

HEARTSONG PRESENTS
HP115—Sisters in the Sun

Crosswinds

Shirley S. Rohde

Heartsong Presents

Dedication
To Kathy, Dawn, and Brad
Three of the best children ever!
And to
Jon, Tom, and Kelly
Who complete the circle.

A note from the Author:
I love to hear from my readers! You may write to me at
the following address: **Shirley S. Rohde**
Author Relations
P.O. Box 719
Uhrichsville, OH 44683

ISBN 1-57748-013-9

CROSSWINDS

Cover illustration by Victoria Lisi and Juilius.

PRINTED IN THE U.S.A.

one

Annette's hand dropped so slowly to her side that she was unaware of it. She stared after the train as it snaked down the valley, wrenching her heart with each puff of smoke. She was oblivious to the brush of color enhancing the fall day or the little brick depot with the sign above it swinging in the wind, proclaiming that Schiffley, Pennsylvania was more than a whistle stop. The platform cleared quickly of people after the iron monster had come and gone, taking her husband with it. Yet she stayed, reluctant to go, for leaving the depot meant admitting to herself that Derrick chose to go to war rather than to stay with those who loved him and be amid the security of home and family.

Nettie's heart bounded heavily with the knowledge that Derrick was gone from her life; her throat ached from crying. He had enlisted his services in the beginning of America's involvement in World War I. Europe was another world away. A tremor shook her breath as she thought about his decision to escape their world and the inner turmoil he must have found in it. She tried to be fair. Perhaps he needed to find something in himself. Maybe he simply wanted to be done with their ten-year marriage of one social affair after another, a whirlwind of activity that never quite made for solid wedded bliss.

She was only twenty-six, she reasoned, protesting inside herself. She liked their easy lifestyle, the dances, the parties, the soirees that made her feel like a desirable woman. Still beautiful, if sometimes a little flirtatious, at least there was fun in her life. She could even fit into her wedding gown, a claim not many women her age could make. Her blue eyes clouded and she smoothed a few strands of hair that had come undone under the edges of her stylish feathered hat. Was life supposed to end here as the train carried Derry to some unknown destination? Was there nothing to ever look forward to?

Nettie remembered how she and Derrick were once so much in love and they wanted only to be together forever. Life was wonderful then. Tears stung her eyes; her heart overflowed with love. She must have done something to disappoint him. She was acutely aware that he found no joy in her company nor comfort in her love. He had been preoccupied and restless, even aloof when she had told him her news. Possibilities nagged and weakened her resolve not to cry again.

She walked woodenly toward the Model-T Ford that would take her back to her empty mansion. Ironic that her father had named the huge house after a dream. Her dream had turned downward to a nightmare. When Derrick left, he had offered her the use of his Cadillac but it seemed too cumbersome to drive so she had declined. The groundskeeper had promised he would keep it polished and running, waiting in the garage until he returned. She sniffed. The blue hobbled skirt forced her to wriggle into the seat of the Ford. Her head throbbed; the stitches of guilt knit more tightly until she felt a constricting band about her temples. Days stretched emptily ahead and Nettie found herself envying Derry for at least he anticipated doing something, filling his time and mind. Doubt nagged her. Oh, that she could have it all to do and say over again.

She drove slowly, glad for having to concentrate on the automobile as it ascended the long hill to the Traum. It granted her time before she entered the big empty mansion that her father had built as a replica of the turreted German castles he remembered as a poor peasant boy. It was a gift for his wife at the beginning of the silk mill's prosperity. *Träumerei*, his German word for dream, had been shortened by the townspeople, and the mansion soon became known throughout the area as the Traum.

The silent house cried out for the noise of children and their ceaseless activity. These days there were even few servants to make their presence known. The cook and maid lived in their own quarters and the groundskeeper came and went with the weather or the demand for his services. A family of two had few needs in spite of the large house.

She reached slowly for the doorknob and pushed open the heavy, carved door. Complete silence emphasized her footsteps. The promise of the hush panicked her. Nettie went straight upstairs, knowing her way in the dark, remembering from her childhood which steps squeaked and where the banister had become smooth and worn over the years. Even now in her haste she side-stepped on the wide stairs in her habit of being secretive.

In the cool bedroom she shivered slightly as she tossed her hat onto the dressing table. Unable to hold back any longer, she threw herself across the large canopied bed and burst into sobs that echoed through the night and into the void.

A sound interrupted her weeping. For a moment she listened intently, daring to breathe only short stabs of distress, waiting for the sound to come again. Then she heard it. The turn of a knob; the push of a door. Downstairs someone came into the foyer. In an instant she hurled herself down the stairs and threw herself into the arms of the intruder.

"Oh, you've come back," Nettie sobbed hysterically. "We can make a new life. I will change. . .be all you want me to be. I knew you would come back when you thought it over."

The arms of the intruder, though, did not encircle her small waist. She felt the bulk of his body, the stiffness, the diminished height compared to Derrick's and she recoiled.

The man stood uneasily as she stepped back and peered through the darkness. "Nettie," he said softly.

She ran to the small lamp on a table near the entry and groped for the switch. For a moment she blinked, then recognition steeped color into her face and embarrassment into her wide, blue eyes.

"What is it, child?" Randall Homes stretched out his arms to his beloved daughter-in-law. "You sound distressed. Though there was no light I thought it early for you to retire. I used my key and came in anyway." He tugged at his graying beard in embarrassment.

"Don't apologize, Papa Homes. You know you're always welcome in this house," she said stiffly. Her control crumbled and again she threw herself into his arms. This time he embraced her. "Oh, Papa Homes, what will I do?"

He held her briefly, then stood apart, flushed with emotion and confusion. "Nettie, take hold of yourself and tell me what is the matter. Has Derrick done something to hurt you?" He added sternly, "I'll throttle that boy if he has." He guided her to the settee in the parlor. The room looked more cheerful in the lamplight that shone softly on velvet chairs and damask curtains. "Now, tell me everything," he said kindly.

Nettie took a big breath and loudly blew her nose in Randall's handkerchief. She focused on a photograph on the piano, a likeness of herself and Derrick in happier times. "He's gone," she said at last.

"Gone where,?" Randall snapped impatiently.

"Gone to war," she said simply.

"What?" He wrung his hands, watching her anxiously as she nodded. "You can't mean it." He paced the room in agitation before he sat again and took her in his arms.

"Derry has enlisted. He said he wanted to do something for himself, whatever that means. He said I would understand, but I don't. It didn't even matter when I told him. . ." She broke into hysterical, racking sobs that made her words unintelligible. She tried to make herself understood again. "All he could say was, 'The die is cast. There is no turning back.' "

Homes fumed and paced the length of the spacious parlor. At last he calmed himself. Once again he peered down at Nettie. "Tell me more, child." He moaned aloud, unable to contain his pain. "Why didn't the boy tell me he was thinking of going to war?" he wailed.

Tears filled her eyes but she met his squarely. Trying to control her voice, she faltered, "He's not a boy and you must stop thinking of him as one, Papa. After all, he's thirty-one. Perhaps he is gone now because none of us thought of him as a man."

His face contorted and he clenched his fists as the color blanched above his beard.

Her voice quivered again. She commented in the midst of her distraction. "He hates the turrets, says they make him feel like a prisoner in this castle."

"On this house you mean?" He nodded in agreement. "I always found your father's Germanic taste a little imposing myself. Please go on, dear."

"Derry seemed despondent lately. . .deep within himself, moody, not himself. I don't think he liked being in charge of the mill. He often complained about the workers' petty problems. Maybe he felt trapped." Her voice softened to nearly a whisper. "Maybe it is me." She cried softly into the handkerchief.

"Nettie, if Derrick told me once, he told me a thousand times that you were the best thing that ever happened to him. He will always be thankful that Elise saw for herself that you two belong together."

"Why did he go away then?"

"Perhaps it is my fault. I always paid for his scrapes and got him out of trouble. But this mill was the one thing I couldn't undo for him. Your father, God rest his soul, saw to that in his will. But I should have looked for someone else to run the mill for you and your sister and brought him back to the railroad where he belongs. In fact, that's the reason I stopped in tonight."

"You were going to make him an offer?"

"In a way, yes. I've been in Washington all this week. The government has just signed a contract with us to ship men and commodities for the war. I need Derrick desperately. I want him to take his rightful place beside me. Oh, I know I have two sons but it's Derrick I always go to for advice on company matters. He's the more levelheaded of the boys." He paused. "I feel like I've failed him." His gray eyes glistened and he sat quietly holding Nettie's hand. "I need to know where he is, Nettie. Perhaps it's not too late to get him back."

She bowed her head and averted her eyes, the failure heavy on her own shoulders. "I don't remember where he is going. I don't think Derry told me and I was too distraught to ask him. I'm sure he'll be in touch," she added meekly.

Randall pressed white knuckles to his chin. "You must be strong, Nettie. Wherever he is God will bring him back to us and this misunderstanding will be cleared away. I know you have faith, Nettie. I have seen it rise to the top and set your feet on the right path. Pray. The Lord will answer our prayers. I am sure of it. You must believe it, too." He kissed her hand. "Let me know immediately if you hear anything from Derrick."

She nodded with downcast eyes. The difficult times he spoke of were the two miscarriages. It was easy to have faith then; she and Derry shared the sadness and together they could believe in a future. Now, alone, she doubted she could look to God. She did not possess the strength her father-in-law thought she did. Her own father always taught her to make her own way, independent of anyone else, even God.

Tight-lipped and sober, Randall left her standing by the newel post. He muttered something under his breath about using his connections and hurried out into the night.

Surprisingly, solitude did not close in on her when he was gone. This time utter weariness took over and she fell asleep completely clothed as soon as she lay on her bed. It rained and stormed all night and into the next morning but Nettie slept through the deluge. The moment she opened her eyes to a sun-drenched morning, a plan formulated in her head. Her chin stuck out defiantly as she determined she was not Wilhelm Waller's daughter for nothing. That's where she would draw her strength, from the memory of her father. He had been stiff and unyielding until his dying day and only then did he admit to needing God. She put aside her memory of his final acceptance of the Lord. Someday she would have time to sort out her feelings. Today she planned to visit her sister, Elise, who always knew what to do in a crisis.

❧

It had been a long time since Nettie paid her sister a visit. Once again she was unmindful of the rich color in the landscape and when she drove over the crest of the hill, only a short distance from the Traum, she caught her breath. Vibrant slashes of color leapt from the whole countryside below her. Nestled in the center of it sat the large white farmhouse with its green shutters and a long barn, once a stable for expensive horses, but now converted to a shelter for homeless children. Other small, white buildings dotted the landscape; they were Trevor's medical center and various storage sheds and a small stable where Elise insisted on keeping a few horses. Though she never lost her love for the animals, finding time to ride them had become a luxury in her life these days.

As Nettie slowed the Ford and came alongside of the corral,

children of every age and description came running, laughing, and yelling from the shelter. A few she remembered; others waved curiously at the pretty woman who was as much taken with them as they with her. She stopped and permitted them to inspect the vehicle and ask questions. She was demonstrating the gears when her brother-in-law, Trevor, joined them from across the lawn.

"Nettie, how good to see you." He embraced his sister-in-law with his rough tweed jacket scratching her smooth cheek. His rugged style of clothing identified the country doctor; a kind grin and an easy manner added to his air of confidence. Nettie heartily returned the greeting and stared up at him, marveling at how little he had changed since she first met him when they were children. Though he had grayed slightly at the temples, his dark eyes were soft and sympathetic. In all their years he had always been such a good and caring friend. She truly loved him like a brother.

"Papa Homes stopped last evening and told us about Derrick," Trevor told her over the heads of the children. "You must be anxious to see Elise." He smiled easily, showing his even, white teeth and a firm, generous mouth. "At the moment she is feeding, not one, but two infants who just came to us. She set a place out under the trees where she will join you for tea in a few minutes."

"Thank you, Trevor."

He held on to her hand and pulled her close. "Nettie, you know that whatever we can do to help, just whisper it and we'll be there. We love you and pray for you."

"I never doubt your love, Trevor. If it weren't for you and Lise, I would be lost. You may regret the offer though," she teased.

The noisy children, led by her nine-year-old niece, Maribel, grabbed her hands and pulled her across the lawn to the wicker settee. If her heart had raced a little at the thought of facing her sister, she became quickly absorbed into the games of the youngsters. Mischievously they undid the wide sash of her kimono dress and stole the large pins from her upswept hair until it cascaded in heavy, dark gold tresses down her back. Their laughter resounded infectiously across the lawn. Nettie chased them across the lush grass in a game of cops and robbers. When Elise caught up with them, she could hardly tell her sister from the rowdy, disheveled children.

two

Nettie sighed as she took another bite of a dainty watercress sandwich at the small wicker table where she and Elise sat. A gentle breeze fanned the presages of fall. She shivered, warmed by the sun but chilled by the autumn day. "Oh, that the world were so perfect as this lovely setting." She glanced past the long table to the children hastily left to continue their play on the green.

"It *is* perfect, isn't it? Or nearly so, anyway. Sometimes its hard to remember these little orphaned or abandoned children cannot go home to their mothers and fathers at the end of the day. It is so good of you and Trevor to look after them."

"We are extremely fortunate to know such an abundance where there is so much need in the world, Nettie." Laughter bubbled from her lips. "It *is* a full-time occupation, though, and I freely admit it. Sometimes I wouldn't have it any other way. Trevor and I both work at giving each of them some special time away from all the others." Her dark hair was neatly coiled and her face mirrored a look of peace in spite of her many duties. Less fashionably dressed than her sister, Elise looked comfortable in her loose-fitting dress and large white apron. "We also have a few good helpers. Without them this place would be impossible. Last week another county contacted us about taking in some of their homeless children. We're in a quandary trying to decide if we should accept their offer. Oh, there's much to consider." Her face tightened and she grinned mischievously. "I'm so glad you came. I want to talk to you, too, Nettie."

Nettie remained silent for a long time, too preoccupied with her own thoughts to question what her sister had in mind. Elise picked up the conversation.

"Papa Homes said you are sorely distressed, Nettie. Come over to the big swing where we can talk. I can't bear to see you so sad. But, in spite of it, I must tell you, there is a glow about you." She linked arms with her sister and they walked to a wide, two-seater swing shaded by a huge willow tree. Elise shooed away some quarrelsome boys with a mild admonition. "It's our turn to swing, little ones. Run and ask Mary for some of those cookies she helped bake this morning." She laughed indulgently and waved them off.

"Papa Homes told you all there is, I expect," Nettie offered at last.

"I don't see how he could have. Only you and Derrick know what really happened. I don't want to pry, Nettie, but what's the matter with my favorite couple in all this world?" Elise placed a sympathetic hand on Nettie's arm.

Nettie closed her eyes and laid her head back against the green swing. Clenching her fists, she said in almost a whisper, "I have been deserted."

"Nonsense," said Elise shortly and pulled her to an upright position. She stared into the startled blue eyes. "Men have gone off to war since the beginning of time. Countless women have suffered what you are now suffering."

When Nettie chose to be silent, Elise continued. "Though I don't approve of the way Derrick enlisted so hastily, I admire him for wanting to fight for his country. It shows courage and backbone. We *are* in this war, Nettie, like it or not. Trevor and I watched its progression, praying every day that America could escape involvement but it is not God's will apparently. For a long time our country could remain neutral, thanks to President Wilson. Several months ago when the Congress declared war on Germany we were not surprised, just extremely saddened."

"What do people like us know of war, Lise? Why must we be drawn into something not of our doing, so distantly remote from our shores?" She shook her head.

"Nettie, don't you read the papers? Those poor people in England are being denied food and supplies because of the U-boats circling the British Isles. France has been overrun and Belgium besieged. I am not for war but how long can we sit back and watch others suffer? I don't believe in the draft that was approved." Pain darkened her great sad eyes. "What else can they do? Oh, I pray about it and lose much sleep." She sighed and squinted as the sun came out behind a cloud. "I'm sure Trevor would love to join Derrick overseas but the conditions are a little different. He's the only doctor for miles around and is needed here. His deferment papers came just the other day. I admit it was selfish of me to be so relieved."

"But Derry and I never even talked about it. I know he read lots of newspapers but he never confided about the war. I didn't dream it was so bad. I only know he has been so moody lately," Nettie argued. "It seems a completely unnatural thing for him to do."

"Did you think he would be satisfied forever managing a silk mill? When Papa's will was read and we switched places and you married Derrick instead, having Derrick manage the mill was the only solution I could think of and still keep the validity of the will. Now I'm not so sure we did the right thing."

"We have always been so happy." Nettie remembered how determined her father was to insure the continued success of the mill that he had arranged for his elder daughter, Elise, to marry Derrick Homes, the son of a wealthy and successful businessman. Only his death had prevented fulfillment of the terms of the agreement. He never saw how much Nettie and Derrick belonged together.

"Right now, more than ever, Derrick needs your support. Nettie, I promise you, you will be happy again."

Nettie drew herself up indignantly. "Don't make promises you can't keep, Lise. Derry didn't even have the decency to tell me where he is going."

"Trevor and I talked about that. In this area most men are sent to Camp Meade in Maryland. Do you want us to contact the Army for you?"

"No," she nearly shouted. "He must write to me first," she said stubbornly. "I'm not chasing after him."

"Did you argue before he left?"

"No. . .well, yes. I told him. . ." Nettie burst into tears; her heart-wrenching sobs filled the quiet afternoon.

Elise rubbed Nettie's back the way she had often done when they were children and Nettie was upset. "You are with child, aren't you, dear sister?"

Nettie nodded and wept into her hands. When she looked up again, her eyes were red and puffy. "What am I to do, Lise? Even learning I am having a baby didn't keep him home. And he is fully aware of what happened before."

"By the time he had found out he is to be a father it was probably too late to do anything about his enlistment, Nettie. Don't you know that Derrick would never willingly leave you alone at a time like this? He must know such despair to realize he had made a commitment he couldn't get out of. Oh, dear Nettie. For a moment put yourself in his position. I hope poor Derrick has put his dilemma into the Lord's hands. That's what you must do, also." Elise's brow furrowed as she took her sister in her arms and smoothed the dark blond hair until the tears subsided and calm returned.

They sat back at last and looked about the beautiful countryside with the sun filtering through the trees. For the first time Elise began the swinging motion. It was both pleasant and soothing. "And *I* thought to ask a favor of *you*, Nettie."

She smiled and reached out to pat her hand. "You are in no position to grant favors."

"Name it, please. It might help take my mind off of waiting for the post." Nettie leaned forward slightly, glad for something else to occupy her thoughts.

"Well, just before Derrick broke his news to you he came here and asked me to oversee the operations at the mill. I should have realized his talk of going away for a little while meant he was enlisting but I thought he simply meant a business trip. I had no idea it involved months or I would have refused."

"Whatever are you talking about?" Nettie asked curiously.

"I'm saying it badly. It is a matter of going over the books every week and seeing that the operations at the mill run smoothly. Henry Tice is an excellent superintendent and the women love and respect him. It was our good fortune to have kept him on when Papa died. For our own sakes we need to make our presence known at the mill and help iron out any little squabbles."

"Why didn't Derry ask me? I could have done it for him," Nettie said miserably, looking as though she were going to cry again.

"He probably didn't want to burden you and, besides, I am already familiar with the operation."

Nettie shrugged off her answer. "Derry often said the arguments between the help were the worst part of the job. Is this the favor you were going to ask me?"

"Yes, oh yes, Nettie. We are beset by our work with the children and Trevor's practice. If we bring in more children from another county it will burden us greatly. That's what I planned to ask you before I knew you were expecting."

"You must have been reading my mind, Lise. I came here today to ask you if I could find something to do at the mill, though I didn't expect to get the whole responsibility. I need a purpose to my life or I will go mad. I always wanted to learn the operations at the mill but Papa would never hear of it. You know how he felt about working women, except for those who slaved for him, of course. He never put them on an equal basis with us. Besides, you were the one he credited with having a head for business, not me. Derry isn't much different, I guess. He doesn't want his wife to take any part in making a living." She sighed loudly. "Oh, Lise, the house is so quiet I don't think I can stand it. When Inger died a few years ago the mansion felt so empty, like part of our past was missing, too. Even Derry noticed a difference. Now its a thousand times worse." She held back the tears. For a few moments they were silent as they remembered the days of their staunch, German stepmother. She had stayed on in the Traum after Wilhelm's death and had become a friend and companion as never before in their growing up years.

"Perhaps now is not the time to give you this added burden," Elise said thoughtfully.

"Lise, this is the perfect time. Look at you with three children of your own, and still you run this wonderful place."

"Valley Haven," she interrupted. "We finally had to put a name to it because of all the people who wanted to know of it."

"Having your own children didn't stop you from doing something else with your life. The next time I see Derry I want him to know I didn't sit around brooding because he chose to. . .go to war, right in the middle of our lives."

"But you are more delicate than I, Nettie. I've had no problem. . ." It was Elise's turn to blush and stumble on the memory of the miscarriages.

"I agree to listen to Trevor's advice. He can determine if I can fulfill the duties of manager. I promise to abide by whatever he says. Please, Lise, give me a chance. If I find it too tiring, I promise to tell you, honestly." There was more excitement in Nettie's eyes than there had been since the beginning of her ordeal. In spite of appearing tired and strained, her face now registered hope.

Elise considered for a few moments before she spoke again. "There is another condition, Nettie. I insist on it if you are to accept this challenge, and believe me it is a challenge. Women are not readily accepted in the role of management."

Nettie suddenly stepped off the swing into the lush grass and, standing defiantly with her hands on her hips, she glared at Elise. "We must always do things on your terms, Lise. Isn't it enough I am offering to help? I already agreed to abide by Trevor's wishes for the sake of the baby. What more do you want? Why does it always need to be your way?"

Elise held out her hand and looked lovingly at her sister. She pulled Nettie back on her seat. "Not my way, Nettie. Your safety and the baby's are what I am concerned about. I would like to make you an offer. I simply want to loan you my right hand. Do you see Mary Owens in the middle of all the children?" A small woman in a large white apron, not much taller than some of her charges, whirled around in a game and feigned surprise when she was tagged. "She is the one I wish you would take home with you. You won't regret it. The only condition I make is that when Derrick comes home to stay she can come back to us."

Nettie gasped at the offer. She had met Mary before and knew the high regard Elise held for her, though she never got to know her on a personal level herself. She shielded her face in embarrassment. "And to think I practically accused you of wanting to run my life. Please forgive me, Lise. There's only one question. . ." She hesitated.

"You mean Mary's disability? It doesn't keep her from living her life. She has more stamina than I with my two good legs."

Nettie thought a moment as her eyes strayed across the

lawn where Mary played with the children. If they held back when she chased them more slowly because of her exaggerated limp, it was undetectable. Her niece, Maribel, was at the center of the group, vying for Mary's attention. Elise watched wistfully as they often stopped and hugged and held hands between games.

"There is nothing to forgive, Nettie. You've had more than your share of burdens lately. Enjoy the swing while I ask Mary if she will be your companion for as long as she is needed. You are always in my prayers, dear sister." She kissed Nettie's cheek and walked slowly across the lawn where she put her arm about the petite, dark-haired woman who listened for a moment, glanced at Nettie, then walked hand in hand with Elise to the ivy-covered house.

The drive back to the Traum held unexpected tension. The silence was heady with the resentment Nettie felt at last being alone with Mary. During their other meetings she had never taken the time to notice how young and innocent Mary looked, nor did she recognize her enthusiasm for life. Nettie admitted to being piqued over the parting embrace Elise exchanged with Mary and the look of love passing between them when they said goodbye. She also noticed the way Mary lingered by the smaller children and wistfully looked back at them as they drove off. It seemed unreasonable that such a small, unobtrusive woman could be so highly regarded.

"Mrs. Lucas thinks a great deal of your work," Nettie commented after a long silence.

"Mrs. Lucas is my friend. I call her Elise as she wishes, Mrs. Homes. We have worked side by side ever since she and her husband opened the orphanage." She stared straight ahead and added pointedly, "I would do anything on earth for Elise and Trevor. When she asked me to be your companion, I could not refuse."

Nettie stopped the car as the two women confronted each other. "I have never had a companion nor felt the need for one."

"And I have never *been* a companion to anyone," Mary answered. "I am used to working on an equal basis with Elise. She has never treated me as a servant." Her dark eyes flashed while her small hands remained at ease in her lap.

"I understand," Nettie answered tightly as she started the car moving. "Just how did you come to know Elise?"

"She and the doctor saved my life," she said quietly. "I didn't want to speak of my past but since I am to be living in your house I feel compelled to tell you." She slumped in the seat, her mouth fixed in a straight line.

Sensing the difficulty Mary was having, Nettie stopped the car again, this time turning to look directly at her. She reached out her hand and laid it on top of Mary's. For some strange reason Nettie believed this young woman could be her friend if Mary chose not to shut her out.

"Go on, Mary. Whatever it is I will not judge you. I only ask not to be judged in the weeks ahead."

Mary stared at her squarely. "It is not our right to judge, Mrs. Homes, only the Lord's. He is the one we must answer to."

Nettie looked away. "Tell me how you met."

"My husband had just been killed working for the railroad. The track was being laid to connect Schiffley and Allentown. A stick of dynamite exploded unexpectedly and he was buried under an avalanche of dirt and rocks." Her voice trembled but she went on. "The tragedy is in the past and I have come to deal with it. When it happened I didn't want to live with it. . . in fact, I didn't want to live at all. I tried to kill myself in the river. That's when Elise and Trevor came along in their buggy and pulled me out. The doctor risked his life for me, the poor man can barely swim himself. Then, being a healer, he told

Elise what needed to be done. You see, it was freezing cold and he was nearly paralyzed by the ice on his clothing. It was a miracle we both survived." She sat straighter. "So there's my story and the reason I would walk through fire for the two people I love most in this world. They brought me to the Lord, too. Sometimes it takes a terrible act to do that, you know."

Nettie felt some uneasiness in not being able to find the Lord in her own life. Her mother would be appalled though her father would understand. She started the car again and they drove the rest of the way in complete silence. When they entered the house, Nettie ushered Mary into the parlor and lit the lamp. Nettie's brow furrowed with weariness.

"All the way home I tried to think of a way to tell you. . .to ask you to forgive me for being such a snob. It seems all day I have been leaping to conclusions. All these years Elise has been my only true friend even though she is my sister. I sincerely hope you will be my companion and my friend, as well. If I can believe God has not deserted me, and I find that very difficult right now, then I also want to believe He may have sent you to me." She held out her hand to Mary. Without a moments hesitation the woman took it and smiled up at Nettie.

"Elise told me what a wonderful sister you are. I'm happy to be here, Nettie." Together they went upstairs to make preparations for a guest in the mansion.

three

Henry Tice was sympathetic, but not at all pleased. It was as plain as the expression on his wizened face. "Mrs. Homes, your husband left me with the understanding that your sister, Elise, would look over the ledgers and help with any crisis that may arise with the workers. Even her experience is limited in overseeing such an operation. To have *you* take her place is. . .well. . .rather unnecessary. As you know, I do all I can to keep the mill running smoothly. I would be more than happy to act completely on your husband's behalf, thereby freeing you and your sister entirely," he said, puffing his barrel chest out and strutting across his spacious office to a small ornate table that held a cut-glass pitcher of water. Elaborately, he poured a small glassful with his large, thick hands and offered it to Nettie. "You're looking a little pale, my dear."

Nettie fought to keep her hand steady as she reached for the glass. "You are most kind," she said graciously, trying hard to hide the fact she was feeling a little faint. Early on she resolved not to show any weakness in front of Tice. She had to admit he appeared to have a firm hand on the business, but in years of listening to Derrick's complaints about the mill, one comment surfacing on many occasions was his distrust of Tice. His suspicions were never confirmed, however, and as a result he went along for years working with a man he did not like or trust. The thought nagged at her now. If only she had paid more attention to his complaints. Perhaps this was his reason for leaving.

Feeling a clearing of her head, Nettie ended the interview by standing up and saying, "My sister and I have considered

24

the situation at the mill with great concern. We both agreed to the arrangement. Elise is far too busy to spare even a moment of her time just now. I will stop in each afternoon to learn the procedures and meet the employees, Mr. Tice. I'm sure we will get along famously." She smiled up at him and watched his teeth clench in an exaggerated grin. "I expect to take the ledgers with me to study at home. Please, get them ready for me." Her blue eyes gazed confidently at him as her gloved hand extended for his flabby grip.

He dropped her hand like a cold fish. "It has been customary ever since your father's day, Mrs. Homes, for the ledgers to remain in the locked vault and never leave this room, even for examination. You see, all the work is done right here in the mill. That's the way *he* would want it," Tice emphasized.

"Change is good for everyone, sir. Even my father would agree to that," she said firmly, admiring her own audacity to stand up to such an imposing figure. "Today is Friday. I will return Monday afternoon. Have them ready for me, please." She made a small curtsy and forced a smile. For the first time she wondered why Henry Tice had been kept on after her father's death. She did not remember helping to make the decision. Ten years ago she would have been too immature and emotional to even be considered in such a matter. The weight of decision making rested entirely on her sister's shoulders. At that point even Elise probably relied heavily on those already in charge. The past was yesterday. Today Tice, with his sagging jowls and humorless face and pompous manner, was a man she disliked instinctively. Derrick's intuition was probably right not to place total confidence in him.

When Nettie left the building, she leaned against the red bricks, inhaling deeply of the fresh air until her legs felt steadier. She lingered a moment more to feel the warm sunshine on her face. Then she hurried to the car where Mary waited in the driver's seat.

"I expect it will not be an easy transformation, just like Lise said." She sat staring at the imposing factory. "Oh, Mary, I don't know if I can do it. This morning was bluff. I do well with bluster," she said flatly. "It's putting words into action that I'm not so sure about. Mr. Tice is a formidable opponent. It shouldn't be that way but it is. Whether it's because I'm a woman or Derrick let him have his way, I don't know." She laid her head back against the seat and closed her eyes.

Mary patted her hand and gave her a small biscuit before she put the car in motion. "Feeling a little queasy? This should help. Of course, you can do it. It will take a little time but you seem like a perfectly capable woman to me, Nettie Homes."

Nettie chewed the biscuit smiling thoughtfully. "You think of everything, Mary. I never dreamed a bite of food would help quell my uneasy stomach. Nor did I think to change all my appointments for the afternoons when I should be feeling stronger."

"All except this one, I'm afraid. We know Mr. Tice is never in his office Friday afternoons." She concentrated on the road as it narrowed toward the Traum. "I may not have borne a child of my own but I saw Elise through three confinements. It will be to your advantage if Mr. Tice suspects nothing other than that you are a delicate, helpless woman. We know otherwise, of course. It will buy you a little time to learn the operation. Too bad your father never saw fit to teach you about the factory," Mary said. "It's too much to absorb on such short notice. Did you ever consider that Mr. Tice may be bluffing, as well? Next time you go to the office think of him that way. It will give you courage. You might want to pray about it, too." Mary gave her a sidelong glance. "You will be perfectly capable of carrying on the mill until Trevor says stop. What more can be expected of you?"

Nettie laughed and sat back enjoying the cool morning

more than she had hoped. "Tice bluffing, indeed. I like the idea. Mary, whatever would I do without you?"

She laughed. "You won't find out until its time for me to return to Valley Haven and that time will be here before you know it. Besides, you will be very busy by then and I won't even be missed." She grinned broadly as she pulled into the driveway.

For the first time since Nettie had learned she was expecting, she permitted herself to think of the duties and wonder of motherhood.

❧

Nettie's days were filled by poring over strange ledgers with unfamiliar columns of numbers and entries. She met people who had formerly been mere acquaintances. When she could not go to them, they came to her in what seemed an endless stream of salesmen and foremen with charts and graphs that made her head swim and her stomach churn. She complained often and loudly but always found a sympathetic ear in Mary. Her mornings were predictably disturbing, followed by weak tea and a light lunch and a rest period until she recuperated before going to another session at the mill. For the first time since she had begun the trips to the factory, Nettie recognized some progress. She basked in a vague sense of accomplishment; that was why she was so unprepared for Mary's admonishment after a sleepless night.

"Nettie, I must speak to you." Mary sat on the edge of the bed and lifted the cloth from her companion's forehead. "Every night I see you carry a basin of water to your bedside along with a cloth to cover your eyes so no one can tell you've been crying all night."

Nettie turned her back and mumbled some words to the far side of the room.

Mary commanded, "Sit up and look at me, Mrs. Homes!"

Nettie whirled about in bed. For a moment she held her

head before slowly sitting up. "Oh, so now its *Mrs. Homes,* is it? What have I done to meet this displeasure?" she asked icily. "I keep my nose in ledgers all day and bow to everyone at the factory because they are convinced I am an addle-headed twit. On top of which, my whole life has been changed around." Her mouth grimaced in an effort to hold back any further comments she would later regret. She reached for the cloth that had grown tepid.

"Oh, no, you don't." Mary jerked the cloth from her range. "No tears today. You must be strong. I know you're not feeling well and you miss your husband and a thousand other minor things." Mary stood over her with her hands on her hips. "I sympathize with you, Nettie, believe me, I do, but there's only one concern in all your world. . .and in mine."

Nettie stared back at her, blue eyes blazing with defiance. "And what is it, pray tell? And will you report to my watchdog, Elise? When you do, make sure you tell her I did not hear from *Mr. Homes* yet. Tell her she can have this hateful job back. Or better yet, tell her I am turning the whole kettle of fish over to Mr. Tice as he suggested three weeks ago. She likes him, anyway. Why she does is beyond my comprehension."

Mary sat down and put her arms around Nettie in spite of her protests. For a moment Nettie sat stiffly, resisting the embrace but then she laid her head on Mary's shoulder and wept.

"Those are the last tears I will permit, you know. From this day forward we must be concerned with only one important thing. . .for the babe you carry. You must eat well and rest and walk about the grounds and think pleasant thoughts. If you don't get to the mill every day it is no great loss. You said yourself that Tice is capable. Then let him be. On your good days let him know you have not gone away and will continue to be a thorn in his side. The baby, Nettie, the baby, he or she is what really counts. I would pray for him with you—"

"No," said Nettie quietly. "No prayers today." She got out of bed, maintaining her balance before reaching for the draperies to let the morning light into the dim room. From there she walked slowly to her mirror and studied the dark circles beneath her large eyes. She ran her fingers along the puffy curve of her chin. "He wouldn't even know me," she said to herself. Then she turned abruptly to face Mary.

"You are completely right. I am selfish, weighted down by my own problems. This child must be given a chance. I couldn't save the other two even with Derrick at my side. This time I must deliver a healthy child without him to support me. I must, no matter what the cost. Together we will be waiting for him whenever he returns."

Satisfied at last, Mary closed the door to Nettie's room, leaving her to her morning toilette. She stood outside, silently praying for the unborn child, her brow knit with worry. Then she went downstairs where she and the cook voiced their fears over Nettie's chances to go to a full confinement.

&

At Tice's insistence, Nettie sat in a large plush chair in his office as the employees lined up in the hall to be properly introduced. She tried to visualize their stations in the mill as each name and job description was announced by the manager. The men were introduced first since they were higher ranking workers who oversaw the various departments and the running of the machinery. A few of them were familiar to her, having come to the house at various times to consult her father or Derrick on matters of repair and more recently to meet her and explain their part in the operation.

Most of the women were in their teens or early twenties with pale skin and circles beneath their eyes from lack of sleep or poor health. Nettie was appalled by their sameness, their lethargy when they spoke of their duties, their distance as she attempted to say something personal to each one of them. It quickly became apparent they resented her. A few of the younger ones seemed tongue-tied, in awe to meet Mr. Homes's wife. The majority were hard and indifferent, apparently wondering what all the fuss was about. The reaction unnerved Nettie's plans for the nice little chats she wanted to have with the working women. They did not want her or appreciate the effort she was making on their behalf.

The visit dragged on. She felt hot and sweaty, her stomach was unsure if it wanted food or wanted to be rid of it. She wished Mary was here to bridge the gap for Mary had a natural gift with people that Nettie would never possess. But they had decided that first night that Mary's help would be kept to her personal needs. Nettie breathed a sigh of relief when the last woman came through the door. Mr. Tice was called elsewhere and the young woman stood staring at her. She was more sophisticated than the rest. Dark hair framed green eyes that flashed self confidently.

"Mr. Tice didn't give me your name or tell what your station is," Nettie smiled tiredly.

"My name is Florence Higgins. Since I've been here longer than most and know all the stations, they send me where they need me."

"Oh?" Nettie admired the young woman's clear, olive complexion. "That must make you very valuable to the manager."

"It helps," she smiled secretively. "Where is Derrick? Has he gone and left you?"

Nettie sank deeply into the chair. She groped for an answer to the rude question. "Mr. Homes has joined the army. He never mentioned you—" she broke off.

"I bet he didn't. She laughed in a brassy chord. "We had some good times before he went away. I miss him." She pouted with full, painted lips.

"Tell me about your work," Nettie forced an interest even

though her face paled in comparison with Florence's. Her breaths came in exaggerated sameness.

The woman persisted. "That Derrick is quite a kidder. He must keep you in stitches." She punched the air. "I gotta get back to work. If you see him, tell him I asked about him. Just mention Florence. He'll know." She smiled sweetly and turned on her heel and disappeared, leaving a scent of cheap perfume and a vision of flying black hair that both numbed and infuriated Nettie.

For a long time Nettie sat in the high-backed chair, the vision of Florence Higgins embedded deeply in her thoughts. Finally, she rose and stiffly made her way to Mary and the waiting car. On this trip she did not speak all the way home. The consuming question in her mind became why Derrick had really left her. Mary seemed preoccupied with her own thoughts. Nettie was relieved to be spared any explanation of her preoccupation.

❧

Nettie sat up in bed. In spite of Mary's words, words she truly believed, she could not get the picture of the interview with Florence Higgins out of her mind. It weighed her thoughts heavily and no amount of chastising herself for being awake erased them from her mind. This time there was no notion of crying. She tried to take comfort in being unable to weep.

Over and over the same images haunted and provoked her. She replayed the scenes in her mind's eye again and again, ending with Derrick's departure on their last evening together. He had been tight-lipped and pale. His words had been terse, the pitch in his voice so unlike his normal drawl. He had seemed frightened, yet determined in a way she had never known before. Over the years he had often held back vital information from her, problems over the mill, his mother's dwindling health. His worries were always under the surface, as he distanced himself from those around him. Nettie came to accept his need for privacy, recognizing that he drew into himself in a way that excluded even her. On closer examination she admitted in the cold, gray dawn that Derrick rarely confided his hopes and dreams to anyone she knew of, even with his father with whom he had been very close.

She rose quietly and reached for a robe and slippers. Opening the door a crack, she peered into the hall to make sure Mary's door remained closed. She did not want another confrontation.

Tiptoeing down the stairs to the library, she opened the door to the room that had quickly grown musty from disuse with its stores of old books and leather furniture. Derrick had come there only to listen to the crystal set and read the newspapers. Perhaps the answer to his departure was in some way connected to the news of the war abroad that he had always hid from her. She felt loved and protected because he had tried to spare her. The thought nagged her now knowing she had not sensed his pain. "War is not for women," he had told her. "Women must be the patient partners in a marriage and attend to the things in life that really count: home and family."

She shivered against the coldness of the leather chair as she opened the drawers of the desk, rummaging through their contents. There was no purpose to her searching. She longed to find something, anything to put an end to her anguish. It was months since she had come into the library and only then to order a housecleaning and new draperies. Derrick had given instructions that his precious newspapers were not to be disturbed.

The room held many memories, in fact, it had changed very little since her fathers time. Where the inkstand once stood, a table for Derrick's personal things replaced it. He had also added some of his weighty volumes to the leather-bound books. Otherwise, it remained the same. She closed her eyes for a second and inhaled deeply, remembering the smells of her childhood and the ever-present odor of her father's cigar smoke.

Finding nothing unusual in the desk, she wandered to the newspapers, rummaging through front page headings. War headlines leaped up at her. French, British, Russian involvement. It meant so little to her. Realizing the futility of remaining even a minute longer, she started to leave when her eye caught a yellow paper wedged near the bottom of the stack of newspapers. She snatched at it but her fingers could not grasp the corner. She leaned over and separated the sheets and took out a yellow envelope addressed to Derrick. She hurried to the lamp on the desk where she stared at the letter. A skin-prickling sensation raised the hairs on her neck. She hesitated only a second before her shaking fingers delved into the contents. She read in disbelief.

> *Derrick Homes*
> *Schiffley, Pennsylvania*
> *September 16, 1917*
> *This is to inform you that you have been drafted*
> *into the U. S. Army. Report to Fort Meade,*
> *Maryland, on October 5.*

Nettie did not know how long she had sat on the parquet floor. The closing of a door upstairs startled her back to reality; a tightness in her throat brought on violent coughing, followed by an almost hysterical laughing. All this time she thought that Derrick had left her of his own free will. If only she had known that he had been called. She cried in relief, in spite of Mary's admonition. For the first time in weeks she felt free of her pain. The only cloud on the horizon was the conflict she knew would come when she faced Derrick again. In her easement she would not permit herself to entertain any thoughts of Florence Higgins. She ascended the great stairs for her first untroubled sleep since the train had carried her husband far away from her.

four

Derrick fidgeted nervously as he waited behind the other recruits to receive his boot camp pay and instructions for transfer. The six weeks training had been grueling. He was out of shape and unaccustomed to the vigorous drilling and meager provisions of the army. It was clear to him the commanders were trying to cram years of military experience into a relatively short period of time. His mind reeled with new information and the possibilities it represented. He heard the rumors and he believed them to be true. They were going to the Front, that imaginary line between France and Germany. It was the place where American boys were left behind as casualties in a European war that had suddenly become global, all encompassing with its decisions and consequences. A cold spasm gripped his stomach and he fought off waves of nausea. In spite of inner turmoil, Derrick presented a handsome picture in his uniform. He was slightly taller than the men around him, sporting a small mustache the barber permitted him to keep. His eyes were dark and clear and a small scar on his chin added character to his face. The inner turmoil was well-disguised on the outside by his poised manner.

Shouts of joy or denial came from the men as they clomped back through the line. A few were obviously relieved to stay stateside for a few more weeks. Others, more frequent in number, swore or bemoaned their fates as they named the ship that would carry them to France and the Western Front. The majority of those hearing the dreaded news were smooth-faced boys, who quickly became pale, tight-lipped men. Derrick, ten or twelve years older than most of the soldiers, wiped his palms on his wool trousers. The age difference did not make him any less jittery. The back of his neck was cold, then hot. Finally it was his turn to stand by the table and receive the pay envelope and the white slip of paper with his assignment.

He made his way back through a sea of faces before he dared look at the orders. His heart pounded in his chest as he read the instructions of the need for secrecy. The name of the ship glared boldly from the paper. The *Leviathan*. His knees trembled. It was the German warship, *Vaterland*, seized as the spoils of war and now commissioned as a transport for American soldiers. He was granted a forty-eight-hour leave before reporting again. It meant an all-night train ride to see Nettie for a few hours before he would have to leave to assemble with his division in New Jersey from where they would be ferried to New York, the point of embarkation. His head swam. Perhaps it would be the last time he would ever see his beautiful Nettie. He sucked in his breath, leaning against the brick wall of the armory, letting the cold penetrate the back of his khaki uniform. It brought him away from the numbness clouding his mind and made it possible for him to move his limbs again.

Jim Rawley, an acquaintance from the barracks, joined him. "Man, I knew I was going. I never take the lucky draw, never in my life." His hooded eyes glanced nervously at the men passing them as he tried to read in their faces how they were taking the news. "What about you, Derrick?" When Derrick did not answer, Jim commented, "Sure thought you, of all people, would be spared. Don't you own a factory or something?"

"I manage it for my wife and her sister," Derrick said flatly.

"That should count for something," Jim observed. "Couldn't you get a deferment?" His curly hair still kinked in spite of the closely cropped military cut. Though his face held the soft, nearly beardless look of youth, his steely gray eyes added wisdom to his years.

"I probably could have, but I didn't." Derrick commented more nonchalantly than he felt, offering no further information. His deferment could surely have come with impending fatherhood. He went over it a thousand times. Why hadn't he chosen the easy way out when all his life it had been provided for him? It was not fair to Nettie or Elise or his father. He drew in a deep breath and tried to stand straight. If he agonized any longer he would not be able to function. He closed the book on reflecting, recognizing the pain that his decision had brought to his life and the lives of others. He concentrated on the present.

"Where are you headed, Jim?" he asked, suddenly aware of the long silence between them.

"On the *Levi Nathan*," he laughed in a high-pitched, nervous rattle. "That's what the boys are calling the ship. You?"

Derrick nodded. They grimaced in agreement. "I was hoping it wouldn't be so soon. Camp Meade is okay but we sure didn't learn enough to fight a war, now did we?"

"No, we surely didn't," Derrick agreed. "I tried to pretend those weren't real bullets whizzing above our heads. I only bayoneted into the straw in the trench at the right spot once. I would have been dead a hundred other times."

Jim laughed again, but more naturally. "Me, too. Do you think we'll really have to do that? I mean, it will be hard to kill another man, especially with a bayonet, when he's lying there looking up at you." Distaste showed on his face.

The thought already numbed Derricks senses. He nodded in agreement and tried to put it out of his mind. "Are you making a quick trip home?"

"Yeah. I guess I should see my mother and sister once more," he answered with a faraway look in his eyes.

"Don't think of it that way. I'm sure you will see them again." Derrick scolded, surprised at his being able to encourage another man when he felt the same sense of dread.

"Maybe it's what we're all athinkin." Jim gestured to the others milling around the armory.

Derrick nodded. "Each man has his own thoughts today, I'm certain."

"We can ride together as far as Philadelphia, my stop. I'll look for you in Jersey then. Don't miss the boat," he added with a wry grin.

Derrick winced at the intended humor; neither of them laughed. He was glad to share the ride home with Jim for it would be preferable to his own thoughts. But, after Philadelphia he would be on his own and then he would plan on what to say to Nettie. Considering the need for secrecy, it would be very little. First, though, he needed to make peace with her and mend the heartless way he had said goodbye. He blamed himself over and over. Nettie deserved better than he. For the first time in his life he was called to be a man and he had failed miserably. He envied Jim his candor, his ability to bring everything out in the open. They hoisted their gear and boarded the overloaded bus to the train station.

ба

The ride to Philadelphia was monotonous with long, unexpected layovers during which Derrick and Jim took turns dashing out to the depot snack counters, hoping to find sandwiches and hot coffee. Subconsciously Derrick wanted to miss the train on their running stops but logic took over when he realized it would only deprive him of precious time with Nettie.

Contrary to their hopes, the journey did not give them the opportunity to talk. Instead they slept, lulled by the monotony of the swaying train and the dimness in the car at night. When they passed near cities, the lights woke them but rural blackness soon drew its curtain and they went back to sleep. Other soldiers spread their duffel bags into the aisle and rested with loosened boots as they dozed. Only the blue haze of cigarette smoke attested to those unable to sleep.

As they approached the Broad Street station in Philadelphia, they gathered their gear and prepared for the last leg of their journeys, Jim to walk a few blocks to his home and Derrick, to change trains to Schiffley. As Derrick waited alone in the cold gray of dawn, he tried to imagine Nettie asleep in their large cozy bed, her long blond hair tousled, her face smiling in sleep. He longed to take her in his arms and kiss away the hurts of the last few weeks and tell her she would find the strength he knew she possessed. Perhaps she would never forgive him for having left her so abruptly, for not confiding about his consignment. He was not sure he understood it completely himself. For the first time in his life he tried to put himself in Nettie's position.

The ride to Schiffley was unending. The train made every whistle stop and sometimes delayed an hour or longer for reasons known only to the engineer and conductor. Frequently he asked the hour and waited impatiently as the conductor leisurely hauled out his pocket watch and grandly announced the time. Derrick's new gold watch remained in his pocket, though he checked it frequently for the conductor's confirmation. His leave was growing shorter and he hadn't even been home yet. The khaki cap in his hands was folded and creased a hundred times before he lay it on the seat beside him. The car was almost empty; at the distant end another soldier slept fitfully.

When at last his stop was called, Derrick jumped to his feet and quickly collected his bags. Then he stood in the aisle for what seemed an eternity until the final thrust of the train after which the conductor opened the door.

For a few minutes he stood on the platform, drinking in the stillness and the clear mountain air he hadn't realized he missed so much. Quickly he felt the urgency to purchase his return ticket to Alpine Landing, New Jersey. Then he stowed his gear within sight of the ticket master and looked around him for likely transportation home. Behind the platform two men stood talking and smoking against a beat up sedan. They nodded as he approached. One of them, Ed Higgins, a former employee Derrick never liked very much, agreed to take him to the Traum for a dollar. The man had the reputation of being a loafer and an opportunist. If he remembered any of Derrick's distrust of the past it did not show. Higgins talked nonstop, asking confidential questions about the war. Derrick answered evasively, all the while wishing he would be more quiet and his automobile could go a little faster.

Inside the house he was welcomed by a flustered maid who was ready to dash to Nettie's quarters to tell her of his return. Derrick forbade the announcement and was on the second step when Mary came from the kitchen.

"Mr. Homes. . .I mean Private Homes," she blushed.

"Aren't you the young woman who works for Elise?" he remembered.

"Yes, I mean no. I'm Mary Owens." She extended her hand. "Elise asked me to stay with Nettie," she stammered. "She will be so happy to see you. Shall I tell her you're here?"

"Once again, no." He was about to start up the stairs again when he asked, "Is there any reason I shouldn't see my wife?"

"Well, no. She prefers to be left alone in the mornings because of her condition. I was about to go up and see if she's ready for tea. Perhaps I could have cook set a place for all of us."

"All of us,?" he asked stiffly.

"I will eat in the kitchen today," she offered as an after-thought.

"Well see." He took the steps two at a time knocking only briefly before he opened the door.

❧

Nettie lay on a small satin chaise, studying her fingernails. A bottle of smelling salts sat on the mahogany table next to her and a cloth covered her brow. Her face was blanched and she pinched color into her cheeks as she studied a gold hand mirror. Her left hand reached beneath her blue robe to the surface of the chaise and she snatched at the letter she had reread countless times. Only once had she heard from Derrick and then just a brief note to inform her he was all right except for being constantly tired under the barrage of drilling and instructions. There was no explanation of his leaving, or why he had not told her of his notice of draft. The only words to give her any hope that he still cared for her was a hastily scrawled, "I love you," just before his signature. She sighed and the letter slid to the floor as she put her hand across her eyes. She must answer the letter but what she would say puzzled her.

Though the early morning spells of queasiness were coming less frequently, Mary still insisted she continue to pamper herself as a prelude to a busy day. Nettie found herself adjusting to the mill and its petty problems but Mr. Tice was more vocal about her almost daily visits. He resented even the slightest questioning of the ledgers and insisted they were done exactly the same way since her father's days. He always added, "Even Mr. Homes found no fault in my work." Often he loudly harumphed out of the office, leaving her to sit alone until she finally got up and walked about the mill or went home. In her practice of mingling with the workers and chatting with them or simply passing pleasantries, she felt the loss of some of their hostility. She gave the women permission to use her Christian name and found them responding to her in a way that was both heartening and touching. Florence was cool to her but she forced herself to be civil. Tears still came to her eyes when she dwelled on unanswered questions.

Nettie leaned back and thought about the changes in her life since Derrick had left. Her heart ached with memory. On one hand she felt she would never be truly happy again. On the other, she had to admit to liking the new responsibility in her life.

A rap sounded at her door and she lifted her head, expecting to see Mary with her tea tray. The door opened slowly and her hand flew to her lips. She sat up silently, eyes wide as he came across the carpet, more handsome than ever in his uniform.

There was never a moment of hesitation. Nettie flung out her arms. Instantly Derrick was on his knees beside the chaise, weeping in her arms and covering her face and neck with wet kisses. Several moments passed before either of them spoke.

"How could you do this to me, Derrick?" Nettie cried, pushing him rudely away. The dancing blue eyes once welcoming him so warmly now blazed with fury.

"I've asked myself the same question over and over." He refused to meet her cold stare.

"I've been sick and worried and you took time for only this little note," she pointed to where it lay on the floor. She gave him no chance to reply but heaped pent-up accusations onto his bowed head. "I was forced to go begging to Elise, where they have so many children running about they don't know what to do. She could never understand what this child can mean to us. Oh, I am so alone." She cried bitter tears.

"Go ahead, Nettie, hit me, berate me. I deserve it all. You are perfectly right. I am a heel." He sniffed but did not raise his head.

A long silence followed, broken only by quiet sobbing from them both. At last she put her hand under his chin and lifted his face to hers. There was a catch in her voice. "Look at me, Derrick. I must know. . .is there someone else?" Her smooth skin was ashen.

"Oh, my darling, how could you think that of me? All my life I've searched for a woman like you and even when your father destined us for others, I pleaded my case for you. When Elise released me from our troth it was the happiest day of my life. I know what torture you endured, also, so I know you loved me. Love me still, Nettie. There is no one else but you. I beg you to forgive me for leaving so abruptly. My mind was wild to think we could be separated. Then when you told me about the baby I fell apart. I was so torn by duty and obligation I didn't know where to turn. I have taken the easy way out so much of my life. I didn't know if I was man enough to face this. . .I still don't. I am a loathsome coward. I'm so afraid," he mumbled almost incoherently. "If only I had confided in you from the beginning." He carried her over to the bed where they sat together with his arms about her as she cried into his chest.

"Don't cry, Nettie. We have to make each minute count. You must tell me about you and the baby, and Mary downstairs." He glanced over to the writing desk covered with ledgers. "What are they doing here?" he gasped. Then he held up his hand to quiet the answer to his questions and still the anguish in his heart. "Don't answer, my darling. First I will send for a luncheon tray and we will spend our brief interlude together alone, making our world right again."

&

When Derrick slipped quietly out the front door and down the driveway to the garage his steps were leaden with departure, his face was set in determined lines. He glanced back at the house to see Nettie standing by the window with her hand raised in farewell. He tried to memorize every detail of the parting to take with him on the *Leviathan*.

Perhaps she was right when she said they both had some growing up to do. Her words would stay with him, especially those entreating him to put God in his life, as she would try to put Him in hers. He never thought much of praying to God. Although he reserved Sundays for church and making an appearance in the family pew, it was the preacher who said the eloquent prayers, always addressing the sins and temptations of others. Somehow he never identified himself with the messages in those sermons. If only he could find Christ in his own life there might be some peace from the torment he lived with every day. Without realizing it, he said a prayer for Nettie, the baby, and for himself.

At the depot, Derrick was surprised to see the activity on the street and the number of cars lined up in the parking lot. Other infantrymen stood about on the platform, surrounded by loved ones and family. He swallowed hard, conscious of being totally alone. At one end of the station a local brass band blared into the early morning in inappropriate celebration. Women and children waved small American flags. In the distance a whistle heralded an approaching train. Mothers clutched their sons in tearful farewell and swooned into the arms of their husbands when the boys picked up their bags with an air of finality. It was a scene that would be etched forever in Derrick's mind. Death had spared his own mother the pain of seeing her son off to war, but the reality of it all around him weakened his resolve to have courage. For the first time he contemplated the possibility that Nettie might someday repeat the scene with their own son.

For a moment he stood on the bottom step of the train, looking out over the heads of the crowd for a familiar face. Many he recognized. One of the women from the mill, the sister of the man who had given him a lift home, waved frantically to get his attention. He stared at her. Shocking red lips blew him a kiss and her flashing eyes winked. He looked away in embarrassment, glad to be made aware of other men jostling him to move on.

A brief swell of pride replaced the sadness of leaving, a

camaraderie shared with men going bravely off to war with the sights and sounds of support from their home town. He made his way to a seat at the window and looked out over the faces streaming with tears. In an instant his own eyes filled and the heaviness in his chest took over once again.

"Nettie, my beloved Nettie," he whispered against the windowpane as the train started to move.

five

"He was here, Mary. Derry came home and he loves me."
Nettie hugged her pillow to her bosom.

"I never for a moment doubted that he loves you. I've seen
you two together and the adoration is apparent in his eyes."
Mary smiled and sipped her tea. "Too bad it was such a short
leave. Did you tell him about the abominable Mr. Tice and all
the things bothering you at the mill?" She glanced sideways,
knowing full well there was something besides Tice plaguing
her friend.

"No." Nettie closed her eyes and sank back in the bed with
her mouth pinched shut.

"You *did* tell him of your visits to the mill?" She leaned
forward in her chair.

"Oh, Mary, there wasn't time. He saw the ledgers and
when he asked me about them I simply said Elise was going
over them while I rested." She studied the rose pattern in the
quilt.

"Nettie Homes. If there is to be any understanding between
you and Derrick it has got to begin with the truth from both
of you. Everything else will follow." She hid her annoyance
in her teacup.

"When he comes home to stay I will tell him everything, I
promise. Right now he has enough to worry about. He had
to report directly to somewhere in New Jersey. I know from
the look on his face he was dreadfully worried. He is going
overseas but he couldn't tell me where. It was obviously the
reason for the quick leave. I couldn't let him worry about me,
too." Nettie squeezed her eyes shut and wetness seeped from

the lashes. She sat up straighter. "I must think only of the baby. Derry gave me strict orders."

Mary hid a smile.

"I told him we must pray but it has been so long I don't know where to start or even if I truly want to. Sometimes it seems so futile to think God would hear me out of the millions of people on earth."

"We can talk to God in almost any way we choose, Nettie, and rest assured He hears all our prayers. If His answers are not always to our liking we must believe they are made in our best interest. Remember how we pray, 'Thy will be done'? It doesn't have to be formal prayer like the reverend says. Use your own words and just speak to Him. I think they are the best prayers, anyway. He is always there for us no matter how we call on Him. All we must do is welcome Him into our hearts. The rest comes naturally." Mary's hands rested peacefully on her lap. "I know you are familiar with His teachings. I believe you had a good foundation but you have hardened your heart to Him for some reason, Nettie. If you would like, I will lead us in prayer."

"Say them to yourself then. I will pray when I'm good and ready," Nettie answered tartly, turning her face to the wall. She denied having a hardness in her heart, only a longing for her husband. Flinging back the covers, she sat on the edge of the bed and declared, "Mary, get the car and be ready in half an hour." She glanced at Mary in time to see a pained expression on her face. "I'm sorry, Mary. It's just that I can't stop thinking of you as—"

"A servant, Nettie?"

She flopped on the bed again. "I'm doing everything wrong, aren't I? I don't tell my husband the truth and I boss you around. I don't want to pray and Mr. Tice thinks I'm a witch." Consternation lined her fair face.

Mary's mouth crumbled into a smile and a deep hearty

laugh bubbled out of her throat. "You are anything but a witch, Nettie Homes. You are a kind and loving woman, a wonderful sister, and, I believe, a wonderful wife, as well. Otherwise it wouldn't matter a twit if your husband took temporary leave from your side to fight a war. Most important of all, you are going to be a mother and the whole experience makes you see things in a different light. Life isn't always easy but we can have help to get through it. We just have to turn to the Lord and He is there for us. He always knows what to do." Mary sighed and hugged Nettie to her. "The car will be ready when you come down the stairs, have no second thoughts, *Mrs. Homes*." Mary made a snappy salute, then winked one of her dark eyes and quietly closed the door while Nettie sat staring after her, with a frown on her face.

❧

At first glance, operations on the mill floor appeared to be running smoothly. Each weaver watched the precision of six looms, running front to back to see that there were no lumps in the silk threads or defects in the fabric as the machines droned on. Each woman was also expected to twist broken threads and tend to a continuous supply of silk for the shuttles that ran back and forth between the warp threads. It was an arduous job demanding long hours of standing. Floor walkers made their rounds, looking for trouble and keeping a wary eye for the workers they called slackeys. When machines were down for changing to new designs in the fabric, the walkers ran up and down the aisle trying to hurry the tedious job between two women using little wire hooks to fit new threads through tiny holes. Production was not made when machines were idle, they shouted. Tensions mounted; tempers flared. It was not until the sound of smoothly humming machines vibrating the wooden plank floors that the frenzy ceased and the walkers relaxed. The workers went back to the harried job of tending six machines.

Nettie stopped to bide the time of day or exchange some remark with the workers. Some still avoided the greetings, pretending to be absorbed in the silk threads. With practiced effort she recalled their names and said something personal to each one even though she knew they could shun her advances.

Pamela Brady was cleaning lint from an idle machine as she passed. "Oh, Mrs. Homes. How nice to see you again." She made a slight curtsy and blushed beet red.

"It's Nettie, remember? How nice to see you again, Pamela."

"I told my mother of your visits. She said you were from a good family, your mother, of course," she whispered and looked around her in an effort not to be overheard.

Nettie laughed. "My father was good, too, though a bit stiff. Did your mother work for him?"

She nodded. "Her health failed around the same time Mr. Waller, your father, passed away, God rest his soul."

Nettie had no time to question Pamela regarding her mother's opinions of her father, though she often wondered what the employees really thought of him. A whirlwind in a red dress came around a bin of spools, her painted mouth set in a hard line.

"Is the loom ready to be put back into operation, missy? You're costing us money, you know." Florence Higgins stood between Nettie and Pamela, with her hands on her hips and glaring at them both. She looked coldly at Nettie. "You really shouldn't detain the workers, Mrs. Homes. If she doesn't make production I catch the trouble. These women get the notion they're better than the rest of us if you pay them too much attention."

"We were simply exchanging pleasantries, Miss Higgins." Nettie met her on her own level, for the first time conscious of equal height and green cat eyes. "I'm sure a few pennies won't make a difference."

"It will to Mr. Tice, all right. If production falls even a little, he has words with me, and none too kindly, I might add." At such close range Florence was intimidating with her dark beauty and flashing eyes.

In her haste to avoid confrontation, Nettie tried to walk away. Everywhere she turned her path was blocked either by machinery or the woman in the bright red dress who combed slender fingers though her thick dark hair. If she chose to wear it loose and flowing, Nettie assessed, it was only because she was never required to be anywhere near the machinery that often claimed the limbs and untidy hair of the workers.

"I know Derr. . .Mr. Homes was home for a short visit." Her mouth twisted in a sly smile.

"How did you know he was home?" Nettie reeled backward, catching herself on the hard, cold edge of the idle machine.

"I saw him off at the station," she said, smiling smugly. "He was so glad to see me. I even gave him a kiss."

Nettie felt faint. "But he was home for such a short while. I didn't think anyone knew." Her hand flew to her mouth, regretting the words the moment they were spoken. Instant nausea brought a fine bead of perspiration to her upper lip.

Florence gushed sweetly, extending a slender hand that showed none of the toil of Pamela's. "A pleasure to run into you again, Mrs. Homes. You must look me up the next time you come to the mill. You seem a trifle pale. Perhaps your servant should drive you home so you can lie down." She stepped aside to let Nettie pass. "Oh, by the way," she called, "when you write to your husband tell him I sent my regards. On second thought I'll drop him a line myself. I know his address."

Nettie ignored the outstretched hand and stared into the cold green eyes. "Mary is not a servant but a devoted friend.

As for the letter, I'm sure my husband will appreciate any mail from the people who worked for him." With her head held high, she walked past Florence. She was only a few feet away when she heard Florence release a torrent of accusations at Pamela. Her heart went out to the woman for she knew only too well the sting of words. Florence was right about one thing, though, Nettie conceded. All she wanted to do was hurry home and lie down. Once inside the automobile she forced herself to take large breaths until the nausea subsided.

"Well, it certainly wasn't old Mr. Tice who has you so upset. I saw him leave soon after you arrived." Mary made no attempt to start the Ford. Her hand sought Nettie's gloved ones and gripped them firmly. "What's the matter, dear?"

"Oh, a, employee I've been having trouble with. Nothing to concern yourself about." Nettie stared straight ahead and waited for Mary to drive off. She feigned a weak smile. "I thought I was all over this morning sickness, but I guess it will last forever."

"We must make an appointment with Doctor Trevor," Mary commented. "Perhaps it was a bad idea to let you take on such a responsibility." As Mary drove, she glanced frequently at Nettie, her face dark with concern.

Nettie offered no conversation. Occasionally she ran her hand over her abdomen. "We must alter some of my clothing. My waistbands are a little snug and I don't want anyone to know yet. . .not yet." She breathed a sigh of relief and wiped her upper lip on the back of her glove. Her obligation was done for the day. Now her one consuming thought was to run to her room and take out a small picture Derry had given her, the first one of him in his uniform. If it could only give her reassurance to the fears drowning her. The hour and a half she and Derry had spent together would have to last her a lifetime. Perhaps she would never know the answers that plagued her heart and soul.

☙

The Seventy-ninth Division assembled and marched in orderly drill onto the ferry that would carry them across the harbor. There was no time to look for Jim. The lines were forming as Derrick reached the pier. He felt fortunate to not have missed the boat. A wry smile came to his lips. Nothing like being late for a war. Everything the army did to move their men was either early in the morning or late at night. Fog hung over the pier and the foghorns sounded emptily into the gloom.

The ship loomed larger than life as Derrick first glimpsed her waiting in the harbor. For the son of a railroad baron the sight was not an unfamiliar one. All his life he was accustomed to seeing large trains, steamships that transferred goods from the freight cars, huge round houses, and terminals. They were dwarfed in comparison to the *Leviathan* that waited to take him to his destination. A shudder ran through him. He tried to shake it off as he searched the crowd for Jim Rawley.

He turned almost full circle, noting the units forming on the New York pier. He studied the long lines at the tables where men signed safe arrival cards that would be mailed home to their families once the cable came announcing their docking in France. There was always the threat of being torpedoed by a German U-boat before they reached their destination abroad. He was ill-prepared for that and he hoped Nettie would receive the postcard and she would know that he had at least made it to Europe. He almost gave up scanning the crowd when he heard his name being called and saw Jim waving his cap. He was glad for someone who looked for him, someone who knew he was there. It gave comfort amidst his feeling of isolation.

Jim clapped him on the back like he was just as glad to see Derrick. His smile was shaky and few words came in greeting.

He was closely followed by a tall thin man with dark penetrating eyes and a big smile. He did not wait to be introduced but stuck out a hand to Derrick and shook his emphatically. "Jim has told me so much about you, Private Homes. I'm Chaplain Russell Parks. I've been assigned to your division. I'm sure we'll be seeing a lot of each other in the days ahead."

"Pleased to meet you, Chaplain Parks. I can't imagine what Jim was able to tell you. We haven't known each other very long." He glanced curiously at Jim who colored slightly.

"He told me what a fine man you are, taking your consignment when you didn't really need to. That speaks well for a man who puts country above everything else. He also said you were married. It couldn't be easy to leave a wife behind. Any children?" His voice boomed across the heads of soldiers. Several turned to watch and listen.

Derrick wanted to hush him so the others would not hear and think him valiant. "No, no children," he said quietly, knowing he would be confiding in this man about his forthcoming fatherhood and his outright fear and cowardice in going to war. The wool uniform prickled around his neck and sweat ran down his sides. He knew instinctively that the smooth, kind face of the chaplain and his apparent devotion to his profession might bring him the peace he yearned for. Derrick chuckled to himself at the irony. It would take some degree of courage to confess his weaknesses to another man or to God. He wondered at what point he would have the courage. Concentrating on the task at hand, Derrick was glad for the ability to blot out all else. Years of working alongside his father had taught him well.

As quickly as he appeared, Chaplain Parks was gone to some other duty. Derrick and Jim fell in with their regiment and hoisted the heavy bags with all their worldly possessions onto their shoulders. The ramps leading into the ship seemed inadequate for the long line of men who made their way slowly onto the decks. Once on board they discovered strange new sights and sounds on the worthy seagoing vessel that was once the pride of Germany. Obviously even there it had been more than a warship for the transportation of infantry. Lavish appointments and fine polished wood trimmed the decks and attested to more luxurious times. Almost immediately the rumble of the engines told them they were on their way. Derrick experienced panic over knowing his fate was totally out of his hands. Quickly the rush of excitement turned to the familiar dread and he stared out across the open sea, wanting to hold Nettie one more time.

six

Nettie sat bolt upright in bed. Her heart hammered in her ears and sweat drenched her body; her hands shook and damp tendrils of blond hair clung to her neck. She had dreamed Derry was lying beside her and she sensed a fear that enveloped him as he slept. She tried to shake him awake but he did not move. She called out to him and he would not answer. She was still trembling as she reached for the light to make sure he was not lying beside her. Almost simultaneously the baby moved for the very first time. She gasped and felt her abdomen, willing the child to move again. Then she experienced shame to realize he stirred in reaction to her fright, not to the comforting love she wanted him to know. She tried to calm herself for his sake, acknowledging what she knew all along. It was a boy, with Derrick's dark eyes and high brow and manly chin.

Nettie reached for the lamp by the bed. A pain shot down her side and she lay back with a fear as great as the fear that she dreamed Derrick knew. For an instant she was glad she shared the moment with him. Then reason returned and she sank back into her pillows, hoping the pain would not come again. She relived the other miscarriages. This pregnancy was longer by two months. Even Trevor believed she would go the distance this time. The pain did not return and Nettie slept without moving. Her first thought of praying for Derrick vanished with her own discomfort.

When she awoke, movement was easier; a weight had been lifted from her chest. When Mary came into the room with tea, Nettie simply told her of the baby's first movement. Nettie was heartened by the look of relief on Mary's face. She stood by the bed, steadying herself, before trusting to walk to the washstand. She was elated at the almost effortless flow of her body across the carpet. When Mary came to help her, she asked her to bring a hearty breakfast. It was the first time in several months that she felt like eating. When Mary was gone, she sat by the bed, rubbing her abdomen and speaking in low, loving tones to the child. She was going to be all right. *They* were going to be all right. She tried to pray to God, wanting to thank Him for their lives and to ask Him to watch over Derry but the words would not come. Then she lay back, doubting the effectiveness of a prayer spoken out of such desperation. She wanted to weep. She clenched her teeth and swallowed hard. It was not her time to weep.

After breakfast she and Mary pored over the books spread out over the dining room table. Nettie's fingers stopped at an entry made a year after her father had died. It was inconsistent with the monthly statements for profits at the mill. She marked the page with a scrap of paper and put the ledger aside. In the following year's ledger she discovered a similar entry.

"Here's another." Mary brought another ledger to Nettie and they exchanged a look of disbelief.

"There must be a reason there were several months of little profit, Mary. I don't see how Mr. Tice could have made errors. Surely there is a logical explanation. Perhaps a replacement of machinery." Quickly they searched the listings in the months before and after, finding no record of either a new machine or repair.

Mary mumbled to herself.

"What is it? Did you find something?"

Mary hesitated. "Mr. Homes found nothing wrong with the ledgers or he would have brought it to someone's attention."

Nettie sat back, tapping her pencil against the blue cloth binding on one of the ledgers. "I remember him saying that once a year Mr. Tice brought out the ledgers for that year and when Derrick examined it he could never find anything to confirm his suspicions that Mr. Tice was anything but honest. At which point he initialed it as audited. See, here are his initials each November."

Mary gripped Nettie's shoulders. "This is too much for you to even think about, Nettie. You're in no condition. Wait until your husband returns."

Nettie bit her lip. "And what if it doesn't happen, Mary?"

"Don't speak that way," she scolded.

"Men are dying every day. I've seen the list in one of the newspapers Derry subscribes to. What if he doesn't come back?" she asked hysterically. "My son will never know his father."

"Hush, hush." Mary cradled her in her arms, feeling the tension in her body. "Elise and Trevor will—"

"They can't take on another problem," Nettie argued. "I must talk to Elise about the ledgers. She might remember the checks Mr. Tice paid to the estate every month. If only Derrick had confided more to me about the mill. Why do men always think a woman shouldn't be concerned about business?" She was pensive for a moment. "Perhaps I encouraged it. I always relied on him to make the decisions."

"I guess that's the way it is in most marriages. I think your sister and her husband have a rare relationship because they share all of their financial concerns."

"Lise always had a business mind. It comes naturally to her. Even Papa said so." Nettie stood up abruptly, remembering Derry's words. Her head reeled. Immediately she sat again. She tried to calm herself. "Mary, Derry hated going over the books. He said so a hundred times. He liked working with things he could see and feel, like the railroad, not fine silk threads that became cloth for the lining of coats. If only I had realized how unhappy he was." She gripped Mary's arm and stared at her with large frightened eyes.

Mary knelt by her side. "I don't believe for a minute that Derrick was unhappy sharing his life with you, Nettie. You are such a loving, considerate woman. Don't think of it again. I made an appointment for you to see Doctor Trevor this afternoon. You must not upset yourself any further. It would do no good to confront Tice, anyway, until you are certain about your suspicions. I'm sure they can do without your presence at the mill for one day." She smiled and patted Nettie's silken flowing tresses. "Besides, Doctor Trevor should know his nephew is moving about." Then she turned from Nettie to hide the worry that wrinkled her brow.

ð

When Nettie finished her visit with Trevor, she and Mary searched for Elise and led her, protesting all the way, to the cozy sitting room. Sinking into a wing chair, Elise sighed, "This is probably all the rest I will find today. Thank you for rescuing me." She put her hand out to touch Nettie's abdomen. "How is the little fellow?" She smiled and held her arms as though there was a baby in them and crooned as she rocked. "I can't wait!"

Nettie blushed. "Really, Lise!" Then she hastened to add, "Do I really show so much?"

"Only to the trained eye," Elise laughed. "What does Trevor say?"

"He says she must rest as much as possible," Mary interjected. "She's a hard one to keep put. . .thinks that every day she must show her face at the mill."

"Is it really necessary, Nettie?" The concern in Elise's large, dark eyes was echoed in Mary's.

"Some of the workers even expect me now. I think they actually like me," Nettie said breathlessly.

"Of course they do, sister dear. Everyone likes you. How are you and Mary hitting it off?" They laughed together at the intended pun.

"Mary is a gem, though a bit too bossy sometimes." Nettie winked slyly, giving Elise a poke. Then she added, "I don't know how I would survive without her. She keeps my feet on the ground. . .or up in bed." She laughed again to see Mary flush with all the praise.

"Don't forget we want her back at Valley Haven when you no longer need her. Unless Prince Charming comes along before then," Elise teased.

"There are no more Prince Charmings in the world," Mary said. "You married the last one, Elise. And from what Nettie tells me, she has another. What chance does a widow like myself have except to tend someone else's babies?" Mary laughed self-consciously and quickly dismissed the subject.

"Lise, I know how busy you are. . ." Nettie took her cue.

"Never too busy for a visit with my sister."

"I must ask you about the funds we receive from the mill. Do you have a record of what has been received? I've looked through Derry's papers and can't find one.

Curiosity played across Elise's fine arched brow. "Yes, of course, there are records though not here. Because of Trevor's practice and Valley Haven, we hire an accountant who handles all of those things. He also makes the check out to your account when the funds are deposited in the bank each month. Why do you ask, Nettie?"

"I think there are discrepancies in the ledgers, but no proof of wrongdoings at this point."

Elise stared at them. "Surely you don't think Derrick—"

"Oh, no. Oh, no. Not Derry. Perhaps Mr. Tice. . . ," Nettie said weakly.

"But he's been with the mill since Papa was alive."

"But Derry never liked him," Nettie said feebly.

"Nettie, I never liked the man, either, but it doesn't mean he's dishonest. There must be some explanation. However, in order to allay your worries, I will advise our accountant to go over past bank deposits from the mill and give us a complete list. Meanwhile, let's have a cup of tea and put aside all worldly problems while you tell me what you are sewing for the baby and the names you have picked, the room you are fixing up. I want to hear everything."

The intended brief visit stretched into hours. Nettie and Mary left chatting like schoolgirls. Nettie's face was relaxed into a cheerful happy look that Mary had not seen since she had come to the Traum.

&

The landing in Brest, France, after twenty-seven days at sea was beset with tension. Rumor passed quickly among the thousands of soldiers aboard that there were patrolling U-boats delaying their landing and frazzling many nerves. At last they prepared to land. Word was immediately wired to the States so that the safe arrival cards could be sent to the families of the men. Arriving in France was a surprising experience for Derrick and Jim who expected to be immediately transported to the Western Front. For a few days after disembarking, they were paraded like heroes through French villages as the answer to prayers of liberating the country. It seemed such a waste of precious time when the real war was being waged only a short distance away. Finally, after several layovers, they were trucked to a camp in Gillay, miles closer to the front line where they were trained in the questionable art of trench fighting by a team of Frenchmen proficient in the field. It only served to delay the inevitable, Derrick reasoned. He was glad for the added training since he had admitted to feeling inadequate in actual combat during the few weeks at Fort Meade.

His constant companion in off-duty hours was Jim. Sometimes they were joined by Russell Parks, the chaplain, who often sought their company. They came to know and admire the man who would not carry a gun but took up the cross for his countrymen. He treated them as equal comrades and in a few weeks a tight bond formed among the three of them.

Mail finally caught up with the troops just before they were to be sent to the next camp, which was even closer to the front. Jim came waving a packet of letters as they rested in the field before the days march began. Derrick ran to meet him and eagerly snatched the letters out of his hand. They sat on a tuft of ground and tore them open. It was the first mail since they had left American soil. Jim quickly devoured the two pages from his mother and sister and sat watching Derrick.

"You done already?" Derrick grumbled. "Here, read one of mine." He handed him Elise's short note telling of the colorful foliage and Nettie's progress. Derrick had devoured it hastily as well as the one from Mary. Nettie's he saved for last. He smelled the envelope and closed his eyes, remembering the delicate perfume of the woman he loved. At last he opened it very carefully as though trying to preserve every scrap. Around him men fell into line. Still he sat, reading it over and over. He could hardly believe Nettie was selling bonds for the war effort and was visiting the mill, speaking to the women as they worked the line. He was proud of her and relieved she was beginning to confide in him again. She was all right. The baby grew inside her. He wiped tears from his eyes as Jim pulled him into line. Then he carefully folded the letter and tucked it into his breast pocket.

Midway on the march through the French countryside, the men stopped briefly in a field to eat their rations. Derrick took the letter out of his pocket and read it again. It was only after Jim's urging that he took his rations from his pack and began eating. Chaplain Parks caught up with them in the field full of clover.

"I've been hoping the letters reached you. I saw them earlier. You're a lucky man, Derrick. Three letters all at once."

"Oh? And how many did you get?" Jim asked jokingly.

"None," Russ answered quietly.

"Sorry, pal. Maybe they got lost on the way," Jim said apologetically.

The chaplain shook his head. "I would be surprised if one of them had my name on it. I have no family and very few people in my life know my whereabouts."

Derrick stared at him. "It must be lonely for you."

"I am never lonely with God. Just before I was drafted I returned from two years as a missionary to Borneo. There is no time to be lonely in a place like Borneo. God sees to it that every moment is filled."

Jim looked in awe of him. "But wouldn't you like some. . . female companionship? I mean I can't wait to get home and see all the women, especially Josephine, maybe even get married. Isn't a family what you want out of life, too?"

"If it is God's will. I only know that right now, even this very minute, I am filling a need. One day, perhaps."

"Russ, I want you to read a letter of mine. You can answer it, too, if you want. Then you might have something come for you one day." Derrick handed him Mary's letter and pretended to look away as he read it.

"I didn't know your wife was going to have a baby, Derrick." His dark eyes sparkled and he clapped his friend on the shoulder.

"Yeah, ain't that a kick? To get drafted at the same time. Sounds like my kind of luck." Jim slapped his leg emphatically.

"Mary is the young woman who helps my sister-in-law, Elise, with her orphanage. She has agreed to be a companion to Nettie, my wife, during her confinement."

"She sounds like a fine woman," Russ said.

Derrick was the first to respond to the call to fall in line for the last thrust of their journey. It freed him from confiding anything else of himself. He was already feeling vulnerable by being so close to the Front. From this makeshift camp they could hear the boom of cannons in the distance.

Two more hours of arduous marching through hilly villages where townspeople came out to cheer them on. Jim often broke rank to talk to young French women who spoke no English but smiled and flirted with this handsome young soldier. He ran back into line and waved and whistled as they marched away. "See you in Paris," he always called.

At last they reached the railroad where they were packed into cars like cattle.

Jim joked, "These sidecar Pullmans aren't too accommodating. One of the boys in the next unit said there are eight horses or forty men to a car. How does that grab you, Derrick? They think more of their horses than they do of us."

"That's what war is all about, isn't it, Jim? No one thinks of us doughboys. We can lie down and die for the heads of state and still we get no appreciation for our mundane lives." Derrick fought off waves of nausea as he pressed the letter in his pocket close to his heart. He knew this to be the last leg of the journey and his mind was numb with fear. If only he could tell Nettie. If only he could hold her one more time.

The train began to move. The men jostled together, standing so closely there was no space for anyone to fall over or even bend at the waist. It was simply more evidence of how little infantrymen were considered except for manning the front line. Derrick leaned against the wall and closed his eyes. For the next two hours he tried to blot out all but Nettie's face. To everyone's relief their discomfort was relatively short amid heat and the smell of horses that no one bothered to clean up after since the animals had left.

Finally the train stopped. The door was opened from the outside and the men fell stiffly into rank. There was no delay for rations. A push was made for the Front before darkness fell. The march was through water and mud, then hiking through the thickly wooded paths of the Argonne forest. They knew they were at their destination. The cannons were close. In the dusk the sky glowed red. There was little thought of home as they fell into the long line of trenches. Even hunger pangs were diminished by fatigue.

seven

Nettie threw the skirt and shirtwaist across the room and sat down angrily at her dressing table. Staring at the large pile of discarded clothing on her bed, she massaged her aching back. Only a few pieces still hung in the wardrobe. For the second time that morning she had pushed the hanger to one end of the closet, sorting through the remaining dresses and skirts, one by one, taking each down and holding it across her widening belly. And one more time she had reached the end of the rod without finding one garment to fit. She kicked a shoe under the bed and hurled a crumbled dress after it. Then she returned to the dressing table bench and held her head in her hands and fought back tears.

"I must not weep, I must not weep," she told herself.

Mary's gentle knock sounded on the door followed by the customary pause. The door opened and she stuck her head into the room, her large dark eyes riveted on the mound of clothing. She stifled a chuckle and pushed the door wide open. "Whatever is the matter, dear? Doesn't anything fit?" She hurried to where Nettie sat, twisting a strand of hair.

"I can't go to the mill today. It's no use. None of my frocks fit and I didn't have the dressmaker in to be measured for those dreadful confinement shifts because I don't want the news all over Schiffley. What am I to do, Mary?" Her brow furrowed in a scowl and her lips pursed in agitation.

Mary knelt beside Nettie. "You really should send for the seamstress before the holidays are upon us. The poor woman can't be expected to work miracles and fashion something for you in the twinkling of an eye." She sighed and shook her head. "I was saving my surprise for a Christmas present but I guess this is the better time," she sighed again, rubbing Nettie's back the same soothing way that Elise had always done. "Don't fret, dear, its not a disgrace for a married woman to be in the family way. We thank God you've carried the baby this long and if the world knows it, then so be it."

Nettie looked searchingly into her eyes. "I am thankful, Mary. I do thank God, honestly I do. I didn't want anyone at the mill to know it yet, that's all."

"I would venture to guess most of those women know it already. They're well-schooled in the business of living," she commented.

"Oh, how I wish Derry could be here to see how round I am. I know he would laugh at me, but right now I can't seem to laugh at myself. I miss him so."

"I know you do, dearest Nettie. You did all you can do for Derrick when you mailed his Christmas package. I know he is in your thoughts and prayers all the time as he is in his friends'. Now you need to do something for yourself. You must accept Elise's invitation to spend the holidays with her family. Perhaps Papa Homes can come, too. It will do you no good to insist on staying here alone on Christmas. Part of the joy of remembering Jesus' birth is sharing ourselves with others. If you don't do it for yourself, then do it for me. I miss my family if I can't spend at least a few hours with them. The children are so wonderful at Christmas." Her face glowed with a rapture that caught Nettie's attention.

"You do miss them, don't you, Mary?"

"Oh, yes. I surely do miss them and all the activity. By now they are busy making gifts for each other and the Christchild."

"What could they possibly make for Him?" Nettie wodered aloud.

Mary smiled with memory. "They decorate the little chapel at the Haven with beautiful paper flowers and garlands they gather from the forest. It's so beautiful. Didn't you ever see it?"

"No, we were always so busy at the holidays with the parties—" She broke off self-consciously.

"Well, then. Ask Maribel to give you a guided tour when we visit the Haven for Christmas. Now, about the present. . ."

Nettie's eyes grew round, then narrowed. "How did you have any time to go shopping? I didn't let you out of my sight for a minute."

"Not all presents come from the department store, Mrs. Homes." Mary gave her a familiar wink and disappeared from the room while Nettie waited in anticipation. When she appeared again she apologized. "I confess my gift is not wrapped so it won't look like a real present."

"Let me see. Please bring it in," Nettie begged, hurrying to the middle of the room. Her hands flew to her face when she saw the garment that Mary carried in her arms.

"I think it's a good color for you. It will show off those wonderful blue eyes," she said holding out a dress to Nettie.

"Oh, Mary. It's beautiful." She took the dress and ran to the full-length mirror where she swayed as if to some imaginary music, holding the blue folds of velveteen in front of her. When she turned to face Mary there were tears streaming down her cheeks. "I can't remember a finer gift nor a more thoughtful one. When did you have time to make it?" She examined the fine stitching in the bodice and on the long sleeves pointing delicately over the wrists.

"I started sewing it the first morning you couldn't come to

breakfast. Elise gave me the fabric several months ago and told me there would be a time I would want an elegant dress. This is the time, my dear. You will wear it with more elegance than I ever could." She laughed self-consciously, blushing at the praise. "I must say as your rest periods became shorter it was more difficult to finish the dress. Cook can tell you how I sat by the fire long after you retired for the night."

"I do thank God for sending you to me, Mary. I don't know how I would have survived without you. You have worked a miracle already. I am talking to God again. Isn't it wonderful?" She glowed with the inner light of an expectant mother. "Thank you for being here, Mary, and for this lovely dress. I will wear it proudly. Your stitches are as fine as those of any seamstress I've ever known." Her eyes met Mary's. "Your gift is from the heart and I treasure it." She reached for Mary and they embraced in a wordless exchange of affection. "I know Christmas is a few weeks off but may I wear the dress now. . .just until I get something more suitable for every day?" She waved toward the pile on the bed. "As you can see, there is nothing I can fit into." Nettie pleaded with her soft mouth curved into a beguiling smile.

"I can see you considered all possibilities," Mary teased. "Of course, you may wear it."

Nettie danced clumsily around the room. "Then please, get the car, dear friend. We are going to the mill and after that we are going Christmas shopping for our stay at Elise's. We must have presents, Mary. We will make it the best Christmas we can." Her blue eyes clouded for a moment. She patted her tummy and spoke softly. "Perhaps your Papa will be home for your first Christmas, my love."

⁂

Derrick and Jim lay in the trench. The sky darkened one

moment and glowed the next with mortar fire. For a while there was a lull and they talked in low tones about how they always spent this night, Christmas Eve. Sometimes their words choked in their throats and they waited in silence as courage came to speak of those times again.

Jim remembered the last Christmas Eve with his mother and sister and her gentleman friend and for the first time, with Josephine. She had joined their celebration timidly. When Jim spoke of her his eyes glistened in the pit when the flares permitted Derrick to see him. He had few words to describe her except she was pretty and dark and of Greek descent. She was not readily welcomed into his family of Presbyterians but Jim was resolute her religion did not matter. His determination won her a place on Christmas Eve and he looked back on it now as no small accomplishment.

Jim asked, "What is the difference in each of us? Aren't we just men fighting for the same cause? Do you think the people at home care which one of us helps bring peace to the world? Would I care if the men up the line are Blacks or Greeks or Catholics or Jews? Why, we could be Latinos or Orientals right now, sitting here in the dark and how would we know? And what would it matter to us or to anyone? If we save each other's lives, won't it count the same in the end?" His angry words seemed to echo through the darkness. When he calmed down he stretched out of his cramped position and his thoughts returned to his woman.

"All I want to think about tonight is Josephine. I'm going to ask her to marry me if I ever get out of this miserable hole. Yes sir, next Christmas we'll be Mr. and Mrs. if I have anything to say about it."

Derrick reached over and clapped him on the shoulder.

"Marriage is a fine institution, Jim. You'll never regret it. I miss Nettie more each day. Its unbearable to be apart. You will know all too well once you've pledged your troth. May you never know separation as a married couple. I hope I am invited to the wedding."

"I never thought of it before but I'd be honored if you were my best man," Jim answered huskily.

"It would be my pleasure." Derrick cleared his throat. It was his turn to reminisce. "Last Christmas Eve we sat in the balcony at church. Nettie was so beautiful in the candlelight. I remember just sitting there listening to her sweet voice as she sang Christmas carols." He leaned forward. "Listen."

All up and down the trenches men's voices filled the air in spite of the shelling. It came as a hushed melody, a quiet singing, almost eerie in quality, but from every sector voices blended in "Silent Night." He and Jim joined in with their comrades.

When they stopped singing Derrick remained motionless, locked in his dreams for a long time. When he regained his voice he spoke almost as though to himself. "Last year we stopped in at Elise's house on our way to a party. The children were so excited. I remember they kept coming to the top of the stairs to ask if Christmas was there yet. Elise and her friends had been busy for months making gifts for the children, not just her own, but all of the children in the orphanage. They even had a crate of oranges shipped in so each child would have one on Christmas morning."

"Just think, next year you and Nettie will have your own little one," Jim said almost reverently.

"I hope you're right, Jim. We already tried and lost two. I wish—" The silence grew heavy as a noise along the line froze them to their guns. They remained motionless until the word "friend" was passed along.

Russ Parks dropped in beside them in the trench and calm resumed. "I've been trying to get through all day," Russ said with some annoyance. "Tonight the captain finally gave me permission to visit the men in the trenches. You two were the fist ones I thought of. Besides, I wanted to deliver this in time for Christmas." He shoved a package into Derrick's stomach. "Glad I won't have to tote that around anymore."

"Most of the men didn't get anything from home. How did I get so lucky?"

They could hear Russ smile in the darkness. "Oh, you and Jim just got lucky because you're personal friends of mine." He slipped a box to Jim. "The rest will have to wait until headquarters hands them out in the morning. A truck made it through loaded with mail and packages. I saw these two and brought them along. At least some of the boys can have a brighter Christmas, thanks to the Red Cross."

The men tore nervously into their packages, waiting for each rocket glare to hold their gifts to the light.

"Shaving soap and a new razor," Jim beamed proudly. "It's from Josephine," he said softly. "I'll read the letter by daylight. Meantime I'll keep it close to my heart." He tucked it into his shirt pocket.

"Nettie made me wool socks. She must have known mine would be in holes by now. My feet are nearly frozen. Wool sure feels good on these cold nights." Derrick looked through the package and half stood to read the words. "I'll save this letter for morning, too. This one's for you, Russ."

"For me?" Russ groped in the dark for Derrick's hand. "It's a present. Surely there is a mistake." He handed it back to Derrick.

He shoved it at him more forcibly. "Look, I nearly got my

head shot off trying to read the name on it. Take it. I thought it might be from Elise, that's why I tried to see the name."

"I can't imagine. . ." Russ tore into the paper and felt the shape of socks with a letter folded into the middle. When the smoke cleared from the last barrage he stood up completely, exposing his tall frame to the light.

Jim pulled him down beside them. "Man, you ain't never gonna get to read it at this rate. Didn't you ever get a present before?"

"Not very often," Russ answered with a low laugh. He sounded almost giddy. "It's from Mary. It's from Mary. I never dreamed. Oh, we have so much to be thankful for this night. We are friends, such good friends. I hope it continues all through our lives. What about you chaps?"

They murmured in agreement.

"I knew it," he said emphatically before he went on. "We even made friends with others. We are alive. We are going to win this war. We are going to return to our loved ones. And more importantly, Jesus Christ is on our side. He is here for us every hour of every day, waking, sleeping. He is watching over us every minute. Let's kneel together and pray for the gift God gave us centuries ago."

Though no fire lit their sky, the men knew a look of total awe glowed in Russ's eyes. They had seen it before when he spoke of the Lord. Between the shelling, in midnight darkness, the three men knelt and held hands and prayed for their blessings and for the coming of Christmas.

&

The day before Christmas, Nettie and Mary both went to the mill. It was unusual for Mary to go but Nettie insisted her friend accompany her to help distribute the gifts she had for each employee. For two days they wrapped the small gifts: a paper bird, a beaded necklace, a scented note pad. They were admittedly small articles but tokens of appreciation, nevertheless. Mary carried two large parcels and followed Nettie into Tice's office as they walked in unannounced.

Nettie stopped short and Mary nearly bumped into her. Henry Tice sat behind his desk with Florence Higgins perched on his lap holding a cup of eggnog. She drizzled sips of pale yellow liquid into his mouth and giggled when it ran down his chin.

At the sound of someone in the room Tice nearly dropped Florence on the floor as he stood up in mortification. "Mrs. Homes. . .we were celebrating. . .eh. . .how good to see you." An embarrassed silence followed as he took in her voluminous blue dress. "I had no idea you were in the family way," he said faintly.

"Well, I did," Florence commented wryly as she hastily left the room.

"Mr. Tice," Nettie colored slightly, "we stopped in today to spread a little Christmas cheer. I can see you are doing quite well without us. Mary and I will see to the employees now." Without giving Tice a moment to respond or explain, Nettie turned on her heel, head held high, and stalked from the office. At the door she paused a moment and looked pointedly back at Tice. "Give my good wishes to your wife sir."

Florence, who was flustered much less then her employer, waited in the corridor. "It was just a harmless little flirtation with the old man," she tried to make light of it.

"You needn't explain to us, Florence. We saw what we saw. It is God you must answer to," Nettie said softly, looking directly into her blazing eyes.

"Look here. I'm telling the truth. Its almost Christmas and we were celebrating. I wanted to make the old man feel good. No use making trouble with his missus."

"I wasn't planning to. I think he sees the light, Florence. I hope you will do the right thing in the future, also." Nettie smoothed her velveteen dress over her protruding abdomen. "A married man is no match for a woman like yourself."

Mary's mouth fell open as the two women confronted each other, one common and arrogant, the other poised and confident. She saw a new side of Nettie, determined and possessive. She realized she no longer spoke of Tice but of Derrick.

"I make no guarantees, Mrs. Homes." Florence gained control of herself and the situation again. "Some married men are not happy no matter what the circumstances." She stared down at Nettie's thickening waist. "Even a baby would not be sufficient to hold some. In fact, it is only a trap." She brushed past Nettie and Mary as she stomped off down the dingy hall.

Nettie paled. Mary did not miss the trembling fingers that flew to her mouth. "Come, let's give out the gifts. We shall rest a few hours before Papa Homes comes to take us to Valley Haven for Christmas Eve."

Nettie murmured something indiscernible as they entered the first noisy room filled with clacking machinery. All over the mill, the workers came forward to voice their appreciation for the first Christmas gift they had ever received from the Waller Mills. For a while the busyness of her role as hostess appeased Nettie and she put Florence out of her mind, but it was not long before fatigue and worry showed on her lovely face.

Alone with Mary on the drive home, Nettie lay back against the seat, a look of total submission on her face. Mary worried aloud, "Nettie surely you can't believe a woman like Florence, whatever she has told you about Derrick. When we get home you need to rest and think good thoughts. I don't know what has transpired between the two of you, but you cannot allow yourself to believe a word of her contrived stories."

Nettie heard all the words. She knew Derry better than anyone. Once again the child moved violently. She must think only good thoughts, she reminded herself.

She answered Mary lethargically, "When I saw Florence and Tice together I thought my problems were resolved. I pray Derrick finds his way home to me. . .and I believe him when he does. Oh, God, help us." She began to cry and no amount of urging on Mary's part abated the sobs that wrenched her body.

eight

The children finally settled down in their beds, both in the Valley Haven and in the Lucas homestead. Grownups gathered around the large Christmas tree and chatted in small groups as nonalcoholic eggnog and Cook's anise cookies were passed around on silver trays.

"Um," Elise sighed, "I've missed these treats, Nettie. How good of you to share them with us. You look tired, dear."

Mary sat rigidly by her, "I should have insisted you go upstairs when the children were put to bed, Nettie. You know how important—"

"It is to get enough rest," Nettie finished in singsong. "I wish you'd stop treating me like an invalid. If Derry were here we would be dancing around the Christmas tree that Lise and her elves have so beautifully decorated."

"A slow waltz," added Trevor and they all broke into laughter.

"There you go again," Nettie chided good-naturedly.

"Ah, but Mary is right." Randall Homes stood up and held out his arm, waiting for his daughter-in-law to take it. "May I escort you upstairs myself, Nettie? The least I can do for Derrick is to make sure his wife retires at the appropriate time, even at Christmas."

"We're so glad you decided to join us tonight, Papa Homes." Elise hurried to assist Nettie out of the large chair.

Nettie swayed when she stood up. "I feel. . .a little. . . faint." She clutched at Randall's arm and closed her eyes. Everyone ran to help her and carefully lower her back into the chair. Trevor brought his bag and ordered everyone from

76

the room. His examination continued while the family waited together in the kitchen where they huddled around the table exchanging nervous glances.

Trevor's face was drawn when he joined them. "I want Nettie to remain here. We could make room upstairs but she insists on going home to the Traum. Thankfully it is only a few minutes away."

Mary took his arm. Her face showed the same concern as Elises. "What's wrong, Trevor?"

"Mary, I am permitting her to go home only because she has promised to go immediately to bed where you must not leave her side. Make provisions to put a cot in the alcove just off her room where you can spend the night. I'm afraid Nettie is in for a rough time of it if she is to carry this child through the next three or four months. She will probably be confined to her bed for the rest of her pregnancy. . .however long it is."

"Oh, Trevor," Elise cried, "I must go to her."

"Wait, Lise. You must convince Nettie her only hope is to follow my instructions to the letter. Randall, please bring the motorcar around and pad the back seat with comforters while Mary packs the bags she and Nettie brought. Then we can help Nettie into the car and follow you home and help carry her up the stairs."

When the women left, Randall detained Trevor as he was on his way to the clinic. "How bad is it, Trevor? Please, be forthright with me." His face was deeply lined with concern.

Trevor put his arm around his shoulder and looked down into the watery eyes of the man much shorter than himself. "We can only pray for miracles, Randall. It will take one to save the baby and another to save Nettie. God help us that we can save them both."

"Shall I send for Derrick?" he gasped holding his chest. A pained look crossed his face.

Trevor stared straight past Randall's head. After a long

moment he said huskily, "He is at the Front. Though no one has actually said it, I can read between the lines of his letters home. It may take a few weeks to locate him and get him here. No. Give me a few days to see if I can stabilize her condition. Then we can make a decision."

"Let's pray it is not too late, Trevor." Randall walked stiffly past him to bring the car around. He turned his face away to prevent Nettie from seeing the tight-lipped, bitter expression on his face as he helped to ease her into the back seat.

Trevor ran to the clinic for supplies to take along to the sickroom. He was glad no one could see the wetness of his eyes. While he worked, he prayed for the wisdom he would need to save them.

The strange procession drove up the hill to the Traum as midnight church bells heralded in the Christmas Day. It was dark and quiet in the countryside with a few flakes of snow decorating the hoods of the vehicles. Elise embraced Nettie in the back seat of the Cadillac as Trevor and Mary followed close behind. No one spoke. Only muffled sobs came from Nettie. The gravity of the situation emanated from the caravan as it snaked slowly up the hill. Though prayers for Nettie and the baby were silent in the hearts and minds of all, they were so unified in intensity that they called out into the stillness. Below, Valley Haven lay nestled snugly in the dark winter night with Christmas candles in the windows.

The rooms were quickly readied for Nettie and Mary's sleeping arrangements and supplies were brought in to care for a possibly long confinement. Nettie stopped sobbing with the light sedation Trevor had given her. Mary hovered over her, wringing her hands while tears streamed down her face. Randall needed little persuasion to return with Elise to spend Christmas with the children. Their lives assumed a normalcy none of them felt. As a precaution, young Mark Fields from

e Haven came on horseback to keep vigil and be a messen-
r to Trevor in the event he should be needed. Provisions
ere made to send a Christmas dinner and all the trimmings
r those who could not be present at the Haven.

"The first night and the next day are critical, Mary," Trevor
arned. "If the bleeding stops, there might be a chance. Pray.
atch and pray. I'll be back in the morning. I'm sorry you
ust spend your Christmas away from the children. I knew
w much they mean to you."

Mary put her fingers to her lips. "This is a child of God,
revor. I am with them spiritually but I am needed here." Her
es glistened in the lamplight.

"Nettie is fortunate to have you for a friend, as we have
en." He clasped her hand and kissed her cheek. "God bless
u." As Trevor let himself out to the starry night, Mary
elt in her little alcove and prayed.

હ

hristmas for Derrick came and went with little fanfare
cept for the packages from home and some extra rations.
here was no lull in the fighting but, he reasoned, they were
t fighting Christian men. There would be no cause to fight
all men were Christian and committed to God and each
her. For days the army massed the troops. They had not
en told but there was another surge coming or an attack or
an afoot. As Jim would say, he could feel it in his bones.
he cold trickle of sweat ran down Derrick's back again; he
came almost numb with fear. Even Jim sank deeper into
mself, waiting for morning to come. Derrick knew his
ddy was not sleeping by the way he breathed and sighed.
e was moody ever since his declaration about Josephine on
hristmas Eve.

Russ crawled through the darkness and came to the edge
f the trench. "Derrick, Jim, are you awake?"

"Yeah," they grumbled. "What's the word, Russ?" He had

been to see them almost daily since Christmas as though he sensed a need in them both. Even sharing communion in small cave on Christmas Day did not prompt them to speak to him on a personal level.

"I've been given permission to tell the men. At daylight your unit is pushing on to Verdun. The German Army has a stronghold there that we must destroy. I thought you chaps would like a few words with the Lord before the attack." They could not quite make out Russ's blackened face but the gleam of his even, white teeth was visible in the early dawn.

"Yes, Chaplain." Jim reached out for his hand. "I want to be forgiven for my sins." His voice sounded taut, almost cracking with tension and fatigue.

"Let's pray together, Jim," Russ said solemnly. Immediately they knelt together. Derrick listened to a litany of confession and the forgiveness that Russ said God promised to any repentant sinner.

Then Russ crouched by Derrick. "What may I do for you my friend?"

Derrick choked the words out with great difficulty. "I . . . am a total coward, Chaplain. If it weren't for my wife and unborn child I would pick up this gun and end it so I would fight no more." The first time admitting failure aloud was an emotional release he did not fully understand. Sweat dripped from his chin and stood out on the backs of his hands. "I hate this war and the killing and misery I see all around me." He wept unashamedly.

"Derrick, every man here hates being in the midst of a war they cannot understand and want no part of. I'm sure even the captain is afraid, as is every man here. God will carry you through this battle. Whatever His plan for you, it shall be carried out. Be of good faith and know He is with you in your hour of need." Russ gripped his hands with both of his own. "We are in this war to preserve the peace of the most preciou country in the world. If we didn't come to the shores of France, then next time it could be on our home soil with our loved ones in peril. Greedy men know no bounds. They think the whole world is there for the taking."

"In my own fear I guess I forgot what is really important," Derrick admitted quietly.

Jim moved beside him. "I'm afraid, too, Derrick. I guess Russ is right, we all are. I don't expect to—"

"I pray for you, Jim. God go with you. I must confess I am also afraid," Russ said. "But God is my strength and my refuge. He gives me comfort in my human failings. I know He will call me home when my time has come. We do not know the hour or the day. No man does. I am not blind to the possibility of losing my life or those of my friends. That doesn't make any of us cowards."

"Thank you, Russ," Derrick said with a catch in his voice. "I'm glad you found time for us tonight. Go quickly and help some other poor boys the way you have uplifted us. God bless you for being here. May we meet again."

They embraced in silence. Jim and Derrick were left alone to their own thoughts. Prayer was in their hearts but also a calm came with Russ's words. Many described it as the calm before the battle, the acceptance of what could not be changed. Derrick knew it to be something more. It was finding God and knowing He was there in the midst of battle or in the trenches as they waited. His prayers were for his wife and son, the son he knew would surely be his if it was God's will. On Christmas night he had been awakened by a dream in which Nettie's sobs moved him as surely as if she were sleeping beside him. "God, help her," he prayed. "God, give her the Light You have shown me."

❧

Nettie lay despondently in the bed even though Trevor told her that no further bleeding was a good sign. If she stayed in bed for the next three and a half months she would be home free and holding a baby in her arms. She merely stared at him, showing no emotion. Mary tried to interest her in some simple stitching to pass the hours. She simply turned her back and slept.

For two days she rested, barely moving. The morning of the third day she sat up and looked restlessly around the room. "I want to get out of this bed and sit in the chair. I'm feeling fine now. Fetch my robe and slippers." She barked orders to Mary in a way she had not spoken since she had first ordered Mary to bring the automobile around.

"I thank God you are feeling well enough to think about getting up, but Trevor said you are to remain in bed. You agreed to it. I heard you myself. You asked only to be brought home." Mary tempered her words. She sounded defensive. Nettie's ordering her about like a servant cut deeply.

"I had a small problem Christmas Eve. Now I am better. I can sit by my desk and write Derry a letter."

"No," said Mary firmly. "If you wish to write I can bring the lap desk and you may do it in bed."

"You heard my orders," Nettie answered venomously. "Do as you are told."

"You must do as Dr. Trevor instructed or I will go home to Valley Haven where I am needed and wanted." Mary held her ground. Her mouth drew the same determined line as Nettie's. They glared at each other.

A small pillow whizzed by Mary's head. She ducked and collected it and three more and put them within Nettie's reach. "Here's more ammunition. I can dodge faster than you can throw. Go ahead." She stood by the bottom of the bed, flinching with each toss.

With each volley Nettie screamed. "I hate you and your preaching ways. What is your precious God doing for me now with all my prayers? He has abandoned me. I know it.

Well, I can have this baby with or without Him. All your devotions on my behalf were in vain." She laughed hysterically, ending with sobs that wracked her body.

Mary was about to run to her side when a soft knock sounded on the door. Nettie stopped crying and wiped her eyes on the sleeve of her nightgown when Maribel came into the room and hurried to the bedside.

"Don't cry, Aunt Nettie," the child pleaded with deep concern on her little face. "Papa said you might need some cheering up. Because it is winter these are just paper flowers but they are bright colors. I hope they help. The children at Valley Haven made you this bouquet." She handed Nettie the flowers.

Nettie leaned forward and placed her hand on top of the shining brown hair, stroking it lovingly. She brushed the end of a pigtail over Maribel's nose and smiled when the child giggled. "I had a selfish moment," she whispered, averting her eyes from Mary. "The flowers are truly lovely." She buried her nose in the stiff petals and found, to her surprise, a fragrance coming from them.

Maribel's eyes crinkled in a smile. "The pink ones have the perfume. Mama gave us some of her toilette water. I hope you like it."

"Smells delightful. How thoughtful of you." Nettie lay back and basked in the love of the children.

"Mama says we are being tested just like Job was tested. First the well wouldn't work and we couldn't get water for a day and a half, then Mama's favorite horse died. Afterward we had a fire in the chimney and it had to be taken down and there was no heat in the babies' room." She caught her breath and took a gulp of water from a glass Mary handed her. "We needed to find a new place for the babies. Papa's motorcar broke down the day after New Year's, too. But the worst test of all happened when you got sick and couldn't spend

Christmas with us. Are you feeling better now, Aunt Nettie?"

"Much better, thank you, Maribel. I had no idea you were beset by so many problems at Valley Haven. And I went and added to all your woes. You poor child. You must go home and tell everyone I am feeling better and everything is going to be fine. Do you know what I mean, Maribel?"

"Yes, ma'am. The baby is going to come out all right." Her bright eyes studied Nettie earnestly.

Nettie suppressed a chuckle. "I think so. I am going to follow your father's instructions to the letter, make no mistake about it," she promised. "How sweet of the children to remember me with these beautiful flowers."

"Papa said when God got done testing Job He made things better than before. Maybe that's what He is going to do for us."

Mary stepped forward. "I know you are right, dear." She looked at Nettie who quickly looked away.

"If you stop downstairs in the kitchen, Cook might have some of those anise biscuits left from Christmas. Tell her I sent you." Mary bent down and hugged the child. "I miss you. Someday, soon, I will return."

When Maribel left, Mary wordlessly brought the writing materials to Nettie. Then she sat in a nearby rocker and took a letter from her pocket. As Nettie wrote, Mary read Russ's description of the war. Though his letter contained nothing of a personal nature, she felt she knew him from the words he used.

When Nettie finished writing, Mary put a seal to it and placed it on a silver tray on the dresser. In her hurt she did not speak but waited for Nettie to make the next command.

"Mary, please bring the Bible from the bottom drawer. I have such a need to read my mother's favorite passages. I know she has them marked but it's been years since I've read them. Perhaps I can read some of them now." She held out her hand to Mary. "Please, forgive me?"

There was a moment's hesitation. Finally, Mary placed her hand in Nettie's. They made no eye contact; they just touched.

"How am I ever going to convince you I am heartily sorry? I have been so impossible, fighting you every step of the way. There will be no baby unless God wills it. I knew it when I rejected Him. I know it now. Even Maribel recognizes what I would not." She wiped the corner of her eye and tugged on Mary's hand. "Forgive me, dearest friend. Then perhaps you can show me how to forgive myself."

Mary took the book from the drawer. She drew her chair closer to Nettie and looked deeply into her eyes. "There is no need to forgive between friends. I love you, Nettie. Rest assured your sins are forgiven for His sake." Then she opened the book and said, "Your mother has so many passages marked that have to do with faith and tribulations. Do you remember that?"

"Really?" Nettie sat up and reached for the Bible. "That surprises me. She always seemed to have such an enchanted life. . .at least that is my memory of her. I never thought of her as needing assurance of any kind."

"Did you think she was without human failings and doubts?"

"Perhaps I did, but now that I think of how demanding my father was and how she gave up her life as a songstress, it couldn't have all been wonderful, could it?"

"She probably had a great need for faith and strength. She was a strong woman from what Elise told me."

"Let me read for a while, Mary. I need this time alone, please."

Mary nodded. "Call me when you want me, Nettie."

The woman in the bed had a strange distant look in her eyes. She clutched the Bible to her breast and drew a deep breath before she opened it and began turning the pages to read the chosen verses. Words leaped up at her, words to water the faith of a tiny mustard seed. She sighed as she turned to the Old Testament where her mother had circled the Ninety-first Psalm. There she found refuge under the "wings" of the Lord. The terror of her nights seemed a dim memory; her heart was filled with peace.

When Mary peeked into the room some time later, Nettie lay with the open book across her chest and tears streaming down her cheeks. She patted the bed for Mary to come sit by her.

Nettie's voice quivered. "Mary, it was as though my mother picked out the verses I needed to read. So much of my childhood came flooding back to me. I remember some of the words but when I read them. . .really read them, it was like hearing her voice again. It was she asking, 'What are you afraid of. Have you no faith? Oh, Mary, I was like the seed in rocky ground. I thought I had found joy in His word, but when my world crumbled around me, my faith fell away. How could I have been so blind to the truth? Jesus told us there would be tribulations before we enter His Kingdom."

There was a glow in Mary's eyes. "You have been a strong woman in your own right, Nettie. Isn't is wonderful to know He is there for you?"

"Yes," she whispered. "I thought my strength was to stand alone. Now I know I need Someone else. Teach me to pray, Mary. I need to ask His forgiveness and His help to weather this storm. Oh, that I never doubt Him again."

Mary took the Bible in her own hands and turned to Matthew.

"Pray like this: Our Father who art in heaven. . ."

The words came back to Nettie and she joined Mary in the prayer of her childhood, a prayer she had heard in church on those times she and Derrick attended. A new meaning, a new peace came into her heart with the saying of the prayer. They were no longer just words to be repeated. She remembered a phrase from Isaiah that her mother had often said. "And a little child shall lead them."

nine

Under the cover of darkness, Derrick crawled behind Jim through the dusty field. There had been no rain or snow for weeks and the smell of the soil assaulted their nostrils. Derrick held back a sneeze in his khaki coat. The ground was cold beneath him but he pressed on, moving clumsily in his leggings and boots toward the German fortification at the top of the hill. When they were as close as they dared advance to the stronghold without being discovered, they signaled in agreement and simultaneously tossed their grenades into the German bastion. As the blast lit the sky, a barrage of fire came from another German outpost. They flattened to the ground and waited until the next team of soldiers destroyed the fortress firing on them. At various points along the German side of the line, raids were made during the dead of night. Across the terrain the army dug its heels into foreign soil.

Derrick and Jim were the first on the mission and had arrived back at their base while the guns still fired at an unseen enemy. "Whew, that was a close one. Why must we always take the first attack?" Jim peered at his bloody hand in the early dawn.

"They didn't nip you, did they?" Derrick sank down at his side and pulled out the small first aid kit assigned to every six men in the trenches.

"Naw, just caught myself on a sharp branch. Now the Germans will have a trail of blood to follow," he complained.

"We must thank the good Lord it's all they will have this night. I hope all the raids won't be this bad. I wonder if the Germans can smell the fear as we start up the hill. I can almost taste it. I try to remember what Russ said about God being on our side, but somehow out there it is so different."

"Don't think of it, Derrick. I know the same fear and it will tear you apart. The important thing is we did what we had to and we returned safely. So I guess Russ was right. God did watch out for us. Try to get a few winks before daylight. I think were in for it then. I figure they'll be fighting mad when they count their dead. How many do you say we lost in this skirmish?"

"Even one was too many," Derrick answered soberly. In his heart he wondered why he had been spared when all around him men cried in pain or were frozen in death. A German soldier cried out in agony after one of the grenades. Derrick was glad for the darkness.

When dawn broke, some of the infantrymen were still returning to the trenches, a few with wounded comrades in tow. A head count was taken, the wounded moved out to the ambulances in the rear, and the massive shelling began again, though somewhat weakened because of the German outposts that had been taken out. The weakness was short-lived, however, as the Germans quickly filled the trenches with fresh troops.

Each night the attack was played out until the Germans fought off the grenades by spraying bullets so thick into the darkness that it was impossible for the troops to rise above the trenches. To add to their frustrations it began raining, first as an easy mist, then a torrential downpour, then it snowed, permitting no movement at night.

Derrick and Jim shivered in the frozen dugout. Mild relief came as overcoats were issued down the line. With them came a stack of letters and they fell silent, reading news from home. Only the noise of the guns reminded them a war was being waged and that they were in the midst of it. Russ's letters from Mary always came inside Nettie's. He looked forward to them and he was nearly always there for mail call. Derrick felt sorry there was only one letter for Russ when he and Jim usually received a packet.

Nettie's letter was the first one since Christmas and he wondered over the delay.

> *All is going well, my darling. You know, of course, I am going to the mill to see the workers. It has been an experience I wish to share with you when you return, for now they look for me and I, for them. Having something to do with my time makes it more bearable while you are away.*
>
> *As for us, my dearest Derry, we are like crosswinds, with an ocean between us, and many unspoken cares and concerns moving back and forth across the sea. Letters can only hint of our longing and our love for each other. Doubts and fears are caught in the winds that blow between us. I pray for the strength to withstand the time and distance separating us. I pray every hour of every day for your safe return. You see, with the help of Mary, I have found God. He is my strength and refuge. I pray you know Him, too. Mary is a good and devoted woman and has been my abiding friend. She and I are devoted to this babe who grows inside me. Together we pray daily for his life and strength. I am convinced it is a boy, with all your endearing qualities.*
>
> *Stay safe and well, my love. I live for your homecoming. Wars drag on endlessly and some men are chosen to go to God, but I know in my heart you will return.*
>
> *Your loving and devoted wife,*
> *Nettie*

Derrick read the letter again and again, amazed that Nettie used the same words about God that Russ had. Her strength and refuge. Oh, to possess their faith. He picked up a letter from his father. In the short message he recognized how deeply hurt his father was by his hasty departure. Nettie had phrased it right. They were at crosswinds: his fathers hurt; Nettie's blaming him for abandoning her, though she never mentioned it in her letters; his own shortcomings by not confiding in them; his floundering faith. He wondered what else was waiting for him at home. Somehow he suspected Nettie had not told him everything. How like her to withhold the truth in trying to protect him. He glanced up just in time to see Russ look away from him. Was there a rise of color in Russ's cheeks? Was it because of Mary or something she told him about Nettie? Derrick felt an uncomfortable, skin-prickling sensation at the back of his neck.

"Foe! Foe!" came the call down the line and each man dropped what he was doing and picked up his gun. Germans were making their way up to the edges of the Allied trenches and in the dawn of a new day they were crawling desperately across the snow in an effort to stem the tide of Americans. There was no time to load and fire. Two men in foreign uniforms jumped into the trench and one of them bayoneted into Derrick's leg. For a second he glimpsed the pointed helmet before he felt the pain.

Moments later he recovered enough to hit the top of the other helmet as the enemy attacked Jim. Immediately, the two Germans were jumped from behind and held down by Derrick and Russ. A third was wounded as he leaned over the edge of the sandbag wall of the ditch and was quickly hauled in and brought to his knees as Jim held the man at gunpoint. The snowy field in front of the line was clear. No more Germans attempted to infiltrate the line. From the lower end of the trench, orders were barked and the prisoners were marched to the command post.

It was only then that Derrick thought of his leg and cleaned the thin trickle of blood oozing from the superficial wound. Russ took him to the field hospital where the wound was bandaged and he was told to return to his station. He walked slowly to his position with a numbing sensation halting his easy strides, but thankful for such a small wound compared to the men who lay helplessly moaning on the stretchers, waiting to be evacuated. He had witnessed the desperation in the young German's eyes as he had fallen into the trench. He was but a mere boy like his cousin at home. For some unknown reason, Derrick found himself praying for the German lad.

Jim handed Derrick the pages of a letter when he returned to his unit. "This was on the ground after the tussle with the Germans. Russ's letter is between the sandbags. He left in a hurry when he took you to the hospital tent. He must be needed because he didn't come back." He pointed to a small hole where they stowed supplies. "I can't imagine those fools trying a stunt like that in broad daylight. It's almost like they wanted to get caught." He shook his head and sat on a sandbag. "I can't wait to get home to a good easy chair." He stretched and tried to conform to the shape of the wall.

"Those men are desperate. Did you see the face of the boy? I have no doubt some of them want to get caught. I don't believe they are being told the truth of why they are fighting."

Derrick sorted through the papers of Nettie's crumpled letter. He stopped and stared at one page with unfamiliar handwriting. In the center of the page a paragraph caught his attention.

> *Nettie has taken to bed on the orders of Trevor Lucas, her brother-in-law and physician. She doesn't want her husband to know this unfortunate turn of*

> *events but because of the seriousness and our deep*
> *concern, I thought it would be better if you knew the*
> *situation. Please, pray for them, Chaplain Parks.*

Derrick was numb with grief. Over and over he berated himself for having left Nettie when she needed him so much. He wiped his eyes with his coat sleeve and felt the burn of cold and dirt. Then he lashed his pent-up frustrations against Russ for not telling him immediately about Mary's letter. He had no right to interfere in something not concerning him. And, last of all, he poured his wrath on Mary. Why didn't she write directly to him? He hit the solid wall of the trench with his fist. His shoulders shook with sobs and he turned away from the men who looked curiously down the line.

While Jim dozed in his contrived easy chair, Derrick slipped the page between the others of Russ's letter. His thoughts ran rampant with the implications of Mary's letter. He debated his next course of action. Logical thought, which was so much a part of Derricks upbringing, took over. Russ would no doubt deny him any further privileged information, which Mary's note surely was. Nettie would keep any news of her condition from him. Perhaps his father could be the link to the truth. In daylight he would write to him. The rest of the long night he dozed restlessly, thinking of home and Nettie.

ॐ

From her upstairs room, Nettie could hear a commotion in the foyer below. She looked nervously at Mary who went quickly downstairs to investigate. She returned, closing the door behind her.

"It seems you have a visitor. We better make you presentable." She began fluffing pillows and arranging covers on the bed.

"Who is it, Mary?" Nettie looked at once excited and flustered. Color returned to her cheeks.

"It's Mr. Tice, dear. I never dreamed he would come down from his ivory tower and sully his shoes," Mary commented more caustically than usual.

"He is here?" Nettie smoothed her hair. "Whatever could he want? The last time we saw him was the day before Christmas when we had that awful scene."

"Exactly. What could he possibly want?" Mary brought Nettie a soft blue bed jacket from a dresser drawer and helped her tie the ribbons.

"Send him in, Mary," she sighed. "I am as ready as I will ever be to see him again." She held up her hand. "He didn't bring Florence along, did he?"

"No, dear." Mary smoothed her hair. "He's alone. I'll be right here beside you."

Nettie lay back and waited. In just a few seconds Mr. Tice was ushered into the chambers. He sat uncomfortably on the edge of a dainty boudoir chair. "We missed your visits to the mill, Mrs. Homes. When I inquired I learned you were indisposed and would not be coming to the mill for some time." He harumphed loudly and studied his large fingertips.

"That is correct," she answered shortly, not offering any conversation to help him through his discomfort.

"Mrs. Homes," he plunged on, "the last time we met there was an unfortunate incident."

"Yes?"

He went on, "A very unfortunate incident as a result of some holiday celebration."

"Yes," she confirmed.

"The matter has my full attention and is completely resolved. Miss Higgins was demoted from overseer to working on the line with the rest of the. . .capable young women. There will be no more indiscretions, I can assure you." Saying that, he stood up and prepared to leave.

Nettie caught him off guard. "And what of you, Mr. Tice?"

Immediately, he sat. The chair groaned. "Me?"

"Yes, you. What have you done about yourself?"

He stared at her, dumbfounded.

"I believe, Mr. Tice, it was your indiscretion as well as Miss Higgins's."

His finger ran the length of his collar. He rose again. "I don't know what you are talking about, Mrs. Homes. I told you the problem was resolved." He stared at the scroll pattern on the headboard.

Mary brought the tea tray she had been sent for and handed a cup to Mr. Tice. He looked nervously from Nettie to Mary.

"I keep no secrets from my friend and companion, Mr. Tice. Also, you may recall Mary was with me when we came into your office."

He nodded, then gulped the hot tea.

"I would like you and Mrs. Tice to renew your marriage vows in front of the congregation. After the renewal you may meet alone on a regular basis with the reverend in whatever work he needs help with."

"But, Mrs. Homes," he protested.

"No one will have to know the reason, Mr. Tice. This will be between the three of us," she smiled. "I wouldn't want to burden my husband with this sort of thing when he returns from the battlefield, Mr. Tice."

"We understand each other completely, Mrs. Homes. I came here today with another concern. I have no idea how long. . .er. . .it will be before you could think of visiting the mill again, but for your own good, I think it best not to come at all."

"Why ever not?" Nettie leaned forward.

"We found walls painted with hateful words, scrawled out against the Germans, probably because of the loyalty your family must feel to that country."

"Mr. Tice, the only loyalty any of us feels is to this great land we live in. Even my father would pledge allegiance to America if he were here." She blinked back hot tears. When she spoke again her words were taut with emotion. "Tell the workers, all of them, that for every Liberty Bond they purchase for the war effort, the Waller. . .no the Homes family will match it dollar for dollar. That should stop the nasty rumors." Then she closed her eyes to blot out his presence.

Mr. Tice bowed curtly. "Good day." With a mighty clatter, he deposited the cup on the tray and stalked out of the room.

Mary and Nettie laughed until their sides hurt at the stricken look on his face. "I'm sure laughter is good medicine, Nettie, but you must be careful not to overdo." Mary was still chuckling when Nettie fell asleep for her afternoon nap. "I wondered how you would handle the situation," she whispered. "Very well, my girl, very well."

᙭

Nettie awoke, perspiring and gasping for air. Vivid memories of the dream persisted. Mr. Tice and Florence Higgins, in a long white gown, exchanging vows in church as she and Justin, her deceased stepbrother, sat stiffly in the family pew and witnessed the ceremony. Derry was not in her dream. She sat up in panic for she dreamed of him every night. It was almost always of his return and him standing before her, ruggedly handsome in his uniform. She cried out in alarm. It had been years since she recalled the tragic fire that had claimed the life of her stepbrother, Justin. Whatever had prompted thoughts of him, she could not imagine. With shaking hands she held the glass of water from her bedside table and drank deeply.

Moonlight flooded the room. Nettie swung her legs slowly to the edge of the bed. She dried the back of her neck with the edge of the sheet and pushed away the damp strands of hair clinging to her forehead. The baby moved as restlessly as she. She stood and walked slowly past the commode, which was as far as she was permitted. The window and the moonlight beckoned just a few feet away.

Outside, the grounds were bare now, the snow gone with the foretelling of early spring. Across the fields Justin's house had been totally demolished but Nettie knew just where it had stood between the oak trees and the rise of land off to the west. She remembered the fire as vividly as though it had just happened. There was a catch in her throat. She was startled when Mary came to stand behind her.

"Cant sleep?" Mary rubbed Nettie's back and brought a shawl to put over her shoulders. "You'll catch cold. You are all wet. You shouldn't be up, you know, dear." Mary guided her slowly to the bed. "Sit on the chair while I change your bed and nightgown, Nettie."

"I didn't dream of Derry tonight. I had the most terrible dream. You don't think it was an omen, do you, Mary?"

Mary glared at her across the bed. "No, Nettie," she said vehemently. "I don't believe in superstitious nonsense. Your dreams are jumbled because you are distressed. God gives us dreams as a way to deal with our problems. Get into bed now with no more talk about nightmares. . .and no more trips. Do I make myself clear?"

Nettie sank into the pillows. "I feel so strange tonight, Mary. It's nothing I can put my finger on, but I know there is something different. Maybe with Derry, maybe with the baby. Oh, I wish I didn't have weeks more to wait." She reached for Mary's hand. "Do you believe this child is heaven sent?"

Mary smiled and stroked Nettie's belly. "All children are heaven sent, Nettie."

"Then how can he not be born healthy? I have truly prayed, Mary. I have offered myself completely to the Lord."

"God hears your prayers, Nettie. He knows we all pray for the boys at the Front and for you and your baby. In good time, my dear. Sleep now. Don't worry about anything. It is all in His hands. Time has been on our side. You will see. Have patience a little while longer, my pet."

Mary sang softly while Nettie fell asleep. Then she turned out the lamp and went to stand by the window where she prayed in the moonlight for Derrick and all the soldiers caught up in the dreadful war, and for a man she was just beginning to know through his letters of faith. But most of all she prayed that Nettie's time had not yet come.

ten

A cry came in the night; the piercing sound stood Mary on her feet instantly. For a second she fought for consciousness before she realized the scream had come from Nettie. Still in her nightgown, she flew to Nettie's side, relieved that dawn's early light showed her the way. Nettie cried out and clutched Mary's hand.

"How long ago since your labor started, dear?" Mary asked more calmly than her racing heart attested to.

"I woke up writhing in pain," Nettie gasped. "Oh, Mary is it time already?" she asked in a weak, shaky voice.

Mary nodded, glad for the respite from pain that Nettie was having. She ran to the pitcher and poured water over a washcloth and wiped her brow.

"Mary, please send for Trevor and my sister. She said she would be here for me. Oh, I want Lise. Please God, deliver this child," she cried out in the midst of another stab of pain.

Mary felt the tautness of Nettie's abdomen. When it relaxed she whispered, "Rest now, Nettie. Mark is in the next room sleeping. I will wake him and send for them both." For a few seconds she hovered in uncertainty as though trying to decide if she should leave Nettie for even a moment. Then she bolted for the door and was surprised to find Mark outside, wriggling into his clothes.

His large brown eyes were round with fright. "I heard the scream and knew it was time to go for the doctor."

"Bring Miss Elise, too. And hurry, Mark, hurry!"

While Nettie was still quiet, Mary ran to her alcove and hastily dressed. She was running a comb through her straggly hair when Nettie called out again. She dropped the comb and ran to her side. "There, there, Nettie. It will soon pass. You must try to rest between the contractions. I sent for Trevor and Elise."

"Why isn't Derry here when I need him? And where is God that He lets me suffer so? Oh, Mary, I'm so afraid."

"Don't be, dearest. Be assured, many women have gone through this and all asked the same questions. It is all part of having a baby. God has not deserted you. He is with you. He will give you strength to carry you through your ordeal. Pray, Nettie, and I am praying, too."

There were times when Nettie slept between the spasms. Mary filled the minutes by accumulating the supplies as Trevor had instructed. She also prepared a small drawer, lining it with cotton and soft baby blankets. It was not yet time. The baby would be tiny. She wrung her hands.

The pains were slowing. Mary stood at the bottom of the bed and watched and waited for another hardening of the abdomen. Trevor came at last. He looked sleepy and perturbed.

"When was the last contraction?"

"Oh, thank God you are here, Trevor." She looked at her small watch on the long chain around her neck. It was one of the things she had grabbed as she dressed so hurriedly. In fact, her nightgown showed beneath the hem of her dress. "They are getting farther apart again. The last was fifteen minutes ago. An hour before they were coming every ten minutes." She whispered, "Oh, I pray you deliver a healthy baby to Nettie. It will kill her, too, if the baby dies." Tears welled in her eyes and spilled over.

"Mary, you and I both know it is in God's hands. I'll do the very best I can with His help. Now, run to the kitchen and tell Cook to set the oven to a low temperature and to boil a pot of water to sterilize some instruments in case I need them. I hope you prepared a place for the baby. If it lives at all it will be very small." Trevor's face was as ashen as Mary's as she hurried from the room.

Nettie awoke with a relatively short pain. She stretched out her hand to Trevor. "Where is Lise? I need her so."

"She couldn't come, Nettie. We have three children down with diphtheria. One of them is critical. . .it's touch and go. She couldn't leave them. Besides, she didn't want to risk bringing the sickness to you."

Nettie stared at him and wailed. "I need Lise. She promised to be here."

He knelt by the bed and took her hand. "Dear Nettie, if you think about it for a moment, you will realize it's for the best. You can deliver this baby without Elise. She sent me because I was taught how to protect myself against these ills. You must make do with me and Mary until things are better at the Haven. Then she will come. She cried when she realized it was impossible. She is having labor pains with you, let me assure you." He sighed. "We have so many problems at the Haven right now. There is a little baby who doesn't want to thrive. . .another child is hopelessly crippled and unwanted. Oh, Nettie, I shall do everything in my power to help you, but the rest is up to the Lord. Have faith, Nettie."

As she slept, Trevor and Mary hoped and prayed for the best and prepared for the worst. Mark hovered in the hall, waiting and watching the comings and goings from the sick room. Then he was given an errand. Solemnly he went riding for Randall Homes.

࿔

Relations were strained between Derrick and Chaplain Parks. Even after careful consideration, a very distraught and emotional Derrick confronted him about the letter from Mary. Russ's face was gaunt with the fresh memory of the wounded and dead, and the endless chain of letters he would be writing to give some form of comfort to their families.

Russ reeled in mild confusion. He scratched his head; a light dawned in his eyes. "I was about to tell you when those Germans jumped into the trench. I'm glad you read the letter. What can I say other than what Mary wrote? I'm not sure why she chose to write to me, except that her concern was so great in case they had to give you bad news about your wife or child. . .or both. It very well sounds like Nettie could lose the child, Derrick. I'm sorry."

"You're sorry? Sorry? I shouldn't be here in the first place."

"You and you alone made the decision, Derrick. If you would like, I'll apply for an emergency leave for you so you can get back to the States. Let me know as soon as you decide."

"It would take forever. Now is when I'm needed."

"Derrick, Nettie is in good hands. You told me her brother-in-law is a doctor. Also, she has found God. What more can you ask?" Russ tried to hide his impatience.

"It may not be enough for Nettie to come out of this unscathed. I told you what she went through before," he complained bitterly.

"Listen my friend. The men I just left, many of them dead, did not have the benefit of a doctor or treatment for their fatal wounds. The living, some of them worse off than the dead, are waiting to be seen by a medic who decides who among them are bad enough to see the only doctor in the next forty miles. You are understandably concerned about your wife but she has her doctor's undivided attention. I feel your pain, but right now I can't look beyond my own. Sometimes I think God asks too much of me. I honestly don't know if I make a difference anymore to these men. I'm being tested beyond my endurance. I feel like Job. I once hoped that you and Jim would hear me out as I have heard so many others. I see I was wrong. There is nowhere I can turn but to God."

Russ's eyes were glazed as he walked past Derrick. There was no promise to return, only his solid footsteps as he walked the short distance to a ditch leading to the command post.

Derrick sank to his knees and buried his head in his hands. Russ's face held such grief and despair. He felt some of his pain himself. He had let his friend down when he really needed him. The memory of his haggard face stayed with him all day.

Later that evening word was passed to be prepared in the morning to be sent back to the reserve units for rest and recuperation. Jim whistled happily as he gathered his canteen and other equipment.

"Aren't you rushing it a bit? There are at least ten hours before we move back. Maybe the Germans have other ideas about our leaving," Derrick said bitterly.

"When they say, 'march,' I want to be ready. What was that all about with Russ? He left in quite a state. He looked like he had just seen a ghost."

"I guess the battlefield is getting too demanding for the man of God."

"You don't mean that, Derrick."

"I do, indeed. Russ is having self-doubts." He regretted betraying the confidence the moment he said the words. He hurried on, "I must decide if I should try to make it home to my wife. She's having a bad time."

Jim whistled again but this time on a note of dismay. "You know how long it took us to get here."

Derrick nodded. "That's the only thing to keep me from bolting out of here. I heard we are being sent back for rest before the big push. Maybe we can all go home soon."

At daybreak, the march began. It was long and hard, over difficult terrain but the French countryside was coming alive with shoots of green and in the fields women planted with their backs bent to the soil. It was a pleasant change compared to staring at sandbagged walls or succumbing to gasses.

All along the line, Derrick looked for Russ as they walked endlessly, then finally stopped to rest in a small forest. Once when an open ambulance passed them filled to capacity, he caught a glimpse of the chaplain holding the hand of a wounded soldier. Derrick's obligation suddenly became clear. Russ was right. Nettie had the solid attention of one doctor helping her, advising her to stay in bed. He could not desert the men or the country who had come to depend on him doing his part.

&

For one whole day Nettie lay without the resumption of her labor and she brightened to the point of denying that she could possibly start labor again so soon. She was more cheerful than she had been in days. When Trevor left to attend to his rounds, he gave Mary his full itinerary lest he be needed. Mark was ordered downstairs for some food before he went back to waiting and sleeping in his room. Even Mary slept, although she could not be convinced to retire to her cot. Instead, she dozed in a rocking chair the few times she could convince Nettie to nap. Downstairs, Randall Homes paced and walked the grounds. He drank black coffee in the kitchen. A guest room had been prepared for him though he never slept in the bed. In his aversion to sick rooms he chose not to visit Nettie but his presence was known in the house.

During the night the labor began again, this time with measured regularity. Mark was sent to get Trevor and the wait began again. Now they were all convinced of the inevitability of Nettie giving birth. By dawn they began to see the crowning of the infant's head. At precisely six o'clock the baby was born and immediately wrapped in blankets to conserve his body heat. The boy was tiny and fragile and made a strange weak cry that at once touched Nettie's heart.

Tears streamed down her cheeks as Mary parted the blankets and permitted her to glimpse the tiny infant in the drawer. Nettie took one of his delicate hands in her two fingers and marveled at their perfection in spite of his size. The baby was quickly whisked from her presence to a table where Mary lovingly placed him, making special effort to jostle him as little as possible.

"Will he live, Trevor?" Nettie raised her head and studied him as he returned from examining the baby.

"I don't know, Nettie. I never saw a baby so small. We will have to keep him by the warmth of the oven and feed him with an eyedropper. Let us hope your mother's milk gives him the nourishment he needs."

"I can't help, can I Trevor?"

"In about two weeks you should be able to go downstairs if you're careful. Mary and Cook will see to him until then. Try not to worry and concentrate on getting your strength back. Everything that needs to be done for the baby is being done. Mary is as good a nurse as any I've found." He straightened his tired back. "The sick children are rallying, thank the good Lord. It looks like they will make a full recovery. Elise can visit you in a few days." He laughed lightly. "So you see, Nettie, we did it without her."

She grimaced. "I would rather she were here, you know." She lay back and snuggled in the covers. "Before I sleep I must thank our heavenly Father. He has brought Billy into this world and I must ask Him to keep him alive now that he is here."

"Billy?"

"I am naming the baby William after my father, Wilhelm. I've changed it to William because, after all, he is not German, but American. My father would be so upset that we are at war with his country. I'm glad he didn't live to see it. Derry will be so proud of his little son."

"One more request before you sleep, and a deserved sleep at that. There is someone waiting to see you. Can you stand a visitor for five minutes?"

"Is it Derry?" she asked eagerly.

Trevor shook his head sadly. "I'm afraid not, but it is someone you love and who loves you very much, your father-in-law."

"Papa Homes?"

"He was here all the time, praying for you."

She wiped her eyes. "I would love to see him and thank him for his prayers." Nettie yawned sleepily. "Have him hurry, please. I'm so tired."

Trevor and Mary left the room together to take Billy to the kitchen. They paused long enough to show Randall his new grandson. Trevor whispered, "I hope Nettie is not being too optimistic. This little fellow has a long way to go before we dare hope. It is now and always has been up to God." He held Randall's and Mary's hands and they prayed together. When Randall opened the door to congratulate Nettie on her fine son, he saw she was sleeping. Quietly he closed the door and walked down the stairs for a breath of fresh air.

⌘

Miles from any action, Derrick relaxed for the first time since the training camp at Gillay. They were permitted to bathe and shave in a heated billet that had once served as a canteen. The men were issued clean clothing and real food, even chocolate bars. Outside they rested in the sunshine while the Red Cross distributed care packages. In the distance they could hear the muffled sound of guns but it seemed years away. Derrick was sure that every man there wished he did not have to return to the squalid conditions on the line but he was just as sure that they would. Rumors were afloat that the Germans were on the run. Long sieges at Badonviller and recent reports from the Luneville sector where doughboys fought side by side with the French to hold battlegrounds and advance on the Kaiser troops did much for the morale. Derrick actually felt a certain pride in his fighting comrades, and in himself. He, also, had helped defend an important line. He tried not to think of what would be asked of them when they returned to the Front.

Jim sauntered over to him, biting into a candy bar. "Guess who I saw in the mess tent?" He did not wait for an answer but blurted, "Russ. He's hoping to join us shortly. Seems as he's been looking for you."

"Good," murmured Derrick. "We need to talk. . .he and I. I must apologize to him. The man was given more than his share and I unloaded on him, too. It was a bad time."

"Funny, but he said the same thing about you."

"He did?"

"On my honor." He lifted his left, then his right hand, laughing all the while. "I think I'm going to catch the first ship home. I'm afraid if I go back I'll never make it to Philadelphia alive."

Derrick said hotly, "You've been saying that ever since we left New York and you're still here, aren't you?"

"And I aim to enjoy each minute." He sauntered off just as nonchalantly as he had joined Derrick. Loudly he called out, "Hey, where are all those French lasses I've been hearing about?" He whistled and strolled off down the dirt road. He did not see the uneasiness in Derrick's expression.

Contrary to the belief that Russ was going to catch up with him, Derrick did not get to meet him until much later. His unit was housed in a makeshift barracks for weeks before their march to another post closer to Paris. A new frustration began when mail was held up, then forwarded, then missed on several occasions when they moved and the mail did not. Morale was low throughout the unit. Derrick and the other men were forced to rely on memories and worn letters, fingered until they were dirty. He was beginning to regret his decision to stay with the troops. All around him was the uncertainty of when they would be called to fight again. He knew the war was escalating. The Germans were on the defensive and the casualties were high on both sides.

eleven

Nettie tossed and turned, unable to sleep with her concern for the fragile baby in the kitchen. In her waking hours Mary assigned Nettie to cut and fold the tiniest of diapers and covers. Each time Mary came into the room, Nettie plied her with questions regarding Billy's feedings, the color of his eyes, the length of his hair, until even Mary came to avoid her trips upstairs. Nettie often fumed in private. Dark circles emphasized her flashing blue eyes. She was nervous and irritable.

Trevor sat by the bed holding her hand. "You know I must start my rounds. There are many patients waiting to see me, really sick people depending on me. Please say you understand if I leave you."

Nettie ignored his pleas and held steadfastly to his hand. "You said Elise will soon be here. When? I'm tired of waiting," she complained. "It seems as though I wait for everything. . .to see the baby, for this dreadful war to end, for Derrick to come home. Oh, Trevor," she threw her head back and rolled her eyes dramatically.

"We have no control over some things in our lives, Nettie. Like the war. I thank God for the dedicated men like your husband. We must concentrate on what we *can* do. We buy bonds, the women roll bandages and knit socks. This is where you come in."

"Rolling bandages?"

"No. By doing what you can do for your private war. By making the best of an impossible situation just the way Derrick is doing in France. Try to hold on to good things.

The baby is taking nourishment, which is a good sign. Every day he survives is a miracle, Nettie. He has your fighting instincts. I have the most wonderful feeling he is going to make it. Keep the faith, Nettie. Hold on to the good things in your life." He poked her shoulder. "Now, you promised me you would get a good night's sleep, and you haven't."

"I can't sleep. All I do is worry about Derry and the baby. Sleep is impossible. I'll be so glad when I can get out of this bed and see a real purpose to my life again." She lay there appearing calm but the constant movement of her hands betrayed her agitation.

"Give it a few more days, Nettie. You are still weak from the loss of blood. Tonight, I promise you, you will sleep. I am leaving a powder with Mary. The children at the Haven are completely out of danger now and Elise is as determined to see you and Billy as you are to see her. I'm not making promises but tomorrow is a new day." He kissed her cheek and hurried out to his motorcar and a list of waiting patients. He was glad he had stopped in to see Billy first.

Nettie's day was filled with myriad chores that Mary had invented for the convalescing woman to do. She was instructed in making bundles of tiny clothing for the baby, filling little bottles with her breast milk for his feedings, and planning Cook's menus for the week. Still, Nettie was not sleepy at bedtime. Mary arrived late in the evening carrying a tray of warm milk and biscuits and the sleeping potion, which she briskly stirred into the milk.

"Trevor is concerned that if you don't get your proper rest you won't be able to relieve Cook next week and give Billy the care he needs." She held the glass out to Nettie who promptly wrinkled her nose.

"I don't care for the idea," she protested quietly.

"Just this once," Mary insisted.

"I promise you, I will sleep."

"It's too late for promises. Drink."

"Mary!" Finally after much deliberation, Nettie took the glass and downed the warm liquid in several large gulps. She made a wry face.

"Good girl. Now I can tell you. Next week we are moving a bed down to the dining room so there will be no need to climb the stairs at night. Then you and I can take care of Billy ourselves."

"Oh, Mary, do you mean it?" Nettie's face glowed sleepily. "Then I can hold him?"

"I'm afraid not. We handle him as little as possible. He's so small."

"Well, at least I can see him." She pulled the covers over her shoulders. "What a wonderful dream I am going to dream, Mary. Thank you." She was asleep before Mary tiptoed across the carpet.

In the morning Nettie tried to rouse herself from the drugged sleep. For a few moments her head swam. The figure in front of her moved and she focused more clearly. Her eyes widened. "Lise," she cried.

They embraced for a long time. "You are the mother of such a perfect little boy," Elise gushed. "He looks just like you. Did anyone tell you that?"

Nettie shook her head and wiped her eyes. The late morning sun played across the carpet.

"He does. He has your pert little nose and dimpled chin. And he has your fair hair, not at all like Derrick's."

Nettie held her hands under her chin in wonderment. "I can't imagine why no one saw it except you."

"Because everyone else has been concerned with his size or his feedings or the fit of his diapers. When I looked at him I saw him as my brand new adorable nephew. And what a love he is." She smiled, smoothing her dark hair that had escaped the coil at the nape of her neck.

"Lise, I am so happy to finally see you. I couldn't believe it when Trevor said you couldn't get away."

"I wanted to come in the worst way. We have such problems, first the sick children, the well, the car, and then the baby." She got up and walked to the foot of the bed. "Nettie, there is something I want to ask you. If I knew of another way I would never think of such an imposition." Her hands dropped helplessly to her sides; her full lips drew themselves into a thin line.

A small cry came from somewhere in the room. Nettie sat on the edge of the bed. "Oh, they *did* bring the baby for me to see. Where is he?" She looked about frantically.

"No, no, dear. It's not your baby. It's little Jamie." She bent down and scooped up a basket with a complaining child tucked in the folds of a blue blanket. "Oh, look at him, Nettie. He is so thin and his color, so pale, it breaks my heart."

For the first time Nettie recognized the pallor and tired lines in her sister's face, and saw how her large brown eyes emphasized the hollows of her cheeks. "What are you trying to say, Lise?"

"This child will surely die if he doesn't get the milk and love of a mother. He was abandoned on the church's doorstep one Sunday morning. I can find no one to take him in. Most of the villagers can barely feed themselves let alone bother about a baby who refuses to eat. Even the women who nurse babies go back to the mill once they get the little ones weaned."

"Are you suggesting. . .?" Nettie tried to stand but sank to the bed again. "I'm sorry for him. . .and you, Lise. I can see you are distraught. I'm sure you did all you could. Don't you see? *I* can't help him. There is a child lying in a little drawer downstairs who is going to need every bit of strength I can muster," she sobbed. "I can't help you. It is too much to ask. Please, take him out of my room. It upsets me so."

"All children are the same in God's eyes, Nettie, even your poor frail child downstairs and this one who can't thrive on his own. They both have God's love and they both want to live." Avoiding her sister's eyes, Elise put a small cape around her shoulders and covered the baby in the basket. "I shall leave him with Mary. She knows what to do. Perhaps you may change your mind and nurse him in the way you can't take your own. He would not deprive Billy of any nourishment because your son needs so little right now. Trevor and I thought you might be willing to try to save Jamie." She drew herself up and kissed Nettie on the cheek. "I must go now. I am sorely needed at home."

Nettie sat there in her nightgown with the edges of the covers drawn around her. Only her bare feet remained on the cold floor. Tears streamed down her face but she was oblivious to all of it.

Maribel ran into the room, excited and rosy cheeked from hovering over the baby's bed by the oven. She stopped short when she saw her aunt.

"Don't be sad, Aunt Nettie. Billy is just beautiful. Even if Jesus takes him to heaven you got to see him and he lived and was happy for a little while."

"What a terrible thing to say, child. I've never been able to hold him except for his tiny hand. And his papa has never even seen him. Don't wish for him to die." Nettie wished this tedious girl had gone with Nettie.

"Mama says if every baby born was as loved as Billy, all the babies in the world would be happy and not just some of them. Jamie isn't very happy. All he does is cry, and such a pitiful little cry. No one wanted him. . .but us. Why do you think it is, Aunt Nettie?"

Nettie stared out the window for a long time. "I don't know, Maribel, I don't know. I will ask God about it."

When Mary came upstairs to look in on Nettie, she found

her sitting on the edge of the bed in a trancelike state. Her hands and feet were as cold as ice. Quickly, she helped her back into bed and rubbed her feet until warmth returned. Nettie stared past Mary as she piled covers on the bed. Satisfied that there was a blush of color returning to her cheeks, Mary busied herself about the room, watching over her. The nagging questions and complaints were preferable to the silence and faraway look in her eyes.

Though it was still early evening, Nettie lapsed into a deep sleep as soon as Mary helped her into bed and put a warming pan by her feet. As Nettie slept, Mary readied the cradle in the alcove for a baby. Quietly, she moved the cot into the hall so it could be taken downstairs in the morning. The cradle was in readiness with all the beautiful covers Nettie had stitched during her confinement.

"Don't you dare put that child in my son's bed," came a thin voice behind her. "And I forbid you to give him any of my milk."

Mary wheeled around and stared at Nettie who stood holding on to the door frame for support. Her pale face matched the solemnity of Nettie's. "So that's the way it is to be again, is it? Your sweet little boy won't need the cradle for some time, Mrs. Homes. I was just going to borrow it for a while. And I wasn't going to give him your milk. You are going to do it yourself."

"In a pig's eye," Nettie said defiantly.

Mary smoothed the vexation from her voice. "Nettie, do you think God wants this child to die if you can save it? Did you ever stop to think that Jamie might be heaven sent because God saw a need in both of you?" Mary put her arm about Nettie's waist and led her to a chair while she proceeded to fix the bed. "You shouldn't be up yet, you know," she said kindly.

"Trevor says I'm weak. I am much stronger than he thinks.

I want to see my baby," she said flatly.

"In the morning when Trevor comes we can ask him about moving you downstairs so you can at least see Billy." Mary's exhaustion showed on her face. "If we move the cradle downstairs, too, it will save me a lot of steps."

"No!" Nettie screamed. "I know what you are trying to do. I know Billy won't be ready for his cradle for some time but I refuse to put a stranger in his bed."

Mary fought back tears. She paused with the doorknob in her hand. "If this were Elise's child you wouldn't think twice about it. I know you, Nettie. I know what a wonderful heart beats inside you. Pray, dear girl. Ask how it is the Lord directs you to do His work. I am needed downstairs now. The works of the Lord are never finished nor would we want them to be. I am so thankful He loves us all in spite of the many times we deny Him." With love in her eyes, Mary looked back at Nettie. Quietly, she closed the door. The irregularity of her faltering steps in the corridor betrayed her fatigue.

ta

Russ caught up with the unit near Paris. He dropped in on Jim and Derrick as casually as though there had not been a falling out. It was plain to see the men were exhausted. The rest that had been granted was an excuse for marching to their next line of defense. Even Russ showed the strains of his duties. All of them languished on makeshift bunks.

"What do you hear from Schiffley?" Russ asked after a long silence.

"Nothing," Derrick answered shortly. "They keep us moving so often there hasn't been any mail for our regiment in weeks. The boys are all grumbling. It doesn't seem fair."

A nerve was struck. For a moment Russ sat up to protest.

"What's fair in war, Derrick?" Jim tried to avoid the argument he saw coming. "Flat out I can tell you—nothing."

"I'm afraid he's right, Derrick." Russ was relieved the comment had come from Jim and not himself. "I have it on good authority that a mule wagon carrying mail got through this morning. The boys who can be spared are sifting through it now. I hope there's something in it for you."

"Don't you mean *us?*" Derrick was on his feet accusingly.

Jim stepped between them.

Russ held up his hands. "Look, you have every right for what you're thinking. I *did* come to see you with the thought that there might be something for me. Whatever Mary writes, you may read, Derrick. I never wanted secrets between us. And don't blame Mary for her concern. I hope Nettie tells you, herself. I pray about it. It was my sincere intention to confide in you before duty called both of us." Russ folded his arms across his chest defensively.

The mail came slowly down the line. Russ waited with the others in the trench. There was only silence, broken occasionally by Jim's snores and Russ turning the pages of his pocket Bible. Derrick was completely into his thoughts.

The packet of mail arrived and Russ waited politely for Derrick to hand him his letter. He read it in silence, waiting for Derrick to finish his own.

"I have a son," Derrick choked out. "Nettie named him William after her father. Not after me, after her father." Tears streamed down his face. "He is so small he has a little drawer for a bed." In his face there was wonderment mingled with pain as he tried to read more from the short letter than the words conveyed. "What does Mary say, Russ?"

"You may read it, Derrick. She simply says your wife is well and can soon take care of the baby herself, along with Mary, of course. She asked me to pray for the child." Russ handed him the letter and stood in the trench, ducking his head. "I'm sorry Nettie didn't give William your name. Perhaps she has her reasons. Don't blame her, Derrick. She is doing her best alone, without you." He knelt down beside Derrick and extended his hand. A mild handshake was given.

"Before I leave, I want to tell you and Jim the latest word from command. It is no secret. We are moving toward Paris. The Germans are approaching from the northeast but the French are planning a big celebration when we get there. Rumor has it that an avenue has been named for President Wilson and each regiment was requested to send a unit to march in a Fourth of July parade. The unit from our division is probably ours. Once again, congratulations on your news, Derrick. I pray for the little lad and your wife."

This time it was Derrick who stood facing Russ. He extended his hand. When Russ took it, Derrick drew him into an embrace. "I'm sorry I blamed you for holding back news, Russ. We need our friends so desperately over here, I can't afford to lose one for even a second. Pray for me, too, Russ. I have never been a father before."

twelve

The first night downstairs for Nettie was unfamiliar, as
though she had not lived there all her life. Although she
would never have admitted to being a creature of habit, seeing
the dining room chairs lined up against the wall and the table
pushed to one end to accommodate her bed, made the room a
stranger to her, as if it did not exist in her or-dered life. Even
the house no longer embraced her sense of family or of
belonging. She tried hard to imagine it as she had become
accustomed to it but the images would not come.

Nettie lay staring at the ceiling where the moonlight cast
eerie shapes and shadows from the wind-blown trees outside.
She raised her head from the pillow and strained to hear if
her son cried out in the kitchen. The only sound came from
the grandfather clock in the foyer. She listened as it almost
measured her heartbeats. She thought again of her precious
sweet baby. She had marveled over him just hours before,
touching his tiny cheek and smoothing the silky light hairs
covering his head. She cherished the memory. Her promise
to Trevor permitted her going downstairs a few days early.
She closed her eyes and thanked God for each day her son
lived and for the privilege of touching him.

A whimper came from the serving area off to the one side
of the dining room and she caught her breath. Perhaps they
had moved Billy closer to her bed. She raised her head and
waited but no other sound came through the semidarkness.
Mary did not stir on her cot in the kitchen. The cry came
again and Nettie was fully awake now. Slowly she slid her
feet to the floor and reached for the housecoat carelessly

tossed over the bottom of the bed.

Quietly she stole to the small serving room and waited by the door. With the moonlight reflecting through the window, she saw the outline of a cradle. Her heart sank for she knew at once it was not Billy. Resentment over Mary's disregard of her wishes, surfaced in her mind. She started to return to bed when the whimper came again. She hesitated for a moment, then walked curiously to the cradle.

In the moonglow the infant flailed his arms and cried weakly. Her heart filled with compassion. She spoke in low, soothing words. "There, there. Don't cry, Jamie. I will get Mary for you." Instinctively she reached out and rubbed his arms and belly until the thrashing eased. She ran her fingers over his head and felt the softness of his downy hair. For a moment she wanted it to be Billy, to take him weeks past the struggle for his life, to be the baby she could pick up and hold.

Nettie bent down and gathered Jamie up and held the child close to her, resting her cheek against his. She sensed his apathy as he lay limp in her arms. She crooned to him and rocked him in her embrace. Her foot brushed against the wood of a chair she recognized as the large rocker from upstairs. Gladly, she rested her shaky legs as she sat down with the baby. Still the child neither welcomed nor protested the arms that encircled him. Nettie wanted to comfort him as much as she longed for comfort herself. She leaned back and rocked. Slowly the baby seemed to nestle against her body.

In a moment when time seemed to stand still, Nettie stopped rocking and undid the front of her nightgown. She opened it and the placed reluctant child at her breast. He was uninterested but lay there passively as she began stroking the side of his cheek. Again he refused to nurse. She sang a lullaby remembered from her childhood and held Jamie with an almost ferocity, so tightly were they bonded. At last the child began to nurse. Great tears of relief ran down Nettie's cheeks and fell onto his little hands. "Now I can weep," she said softly to herself. "At last I can weep." She cried for her son and his absence from her breast; she cried for Jamie and the life surging between them. And she wept for herself and the longing she felt for Derry. Then a great calm took over as she laid the sleeping child in her son's cradle. For the first time since Derry had left she felt total peace. She felt the presence of God as never before.

In the morning Mary spent more time with Nettie than she had since Billy was born. Though she did not see Nettie pick up Jamie and actually nurse him, she knew by his contented sleep that he had found something tangible in his young life, something to hold on to. Nettie seemed different, also. Contentment and calm filled her every breath, her every move. Once a day she would walk to the kitchen to visit Billy where she sat by his bed, all the while talking softly to him and stroking his little body. Then she would go back to the dining room and nurse Jamie when he was brought to her. There was no complaint or criticism. Nettie was a new woman.

"Mary, will you do me a favor, please?" Nettie sat in the rocker, her strength and color dramatically improved. "Will you bring my mother's Bible from the table upstairs. I want to read some of her favorite passages again. I feel so close to her. Isn't that strange?"

"Not at all, Nettie. Elise told me how much your mother loved you both. It is a natural time for a woman to feel close to her mother even if they can't be together." Mary looked away to hide the tears of joy brimming in her eyes. "I believe when Trevor comes to see you today he will grant your wish to spend more time with Billy. I have seen such a change in you the past few days. There is another change, also. Billy's little cheeks are beginning to seem more rounded to me." She smiled with a sense of accomplishment.

Nettie leaned forward in her chair. "Oh, Mary, I hope with all my heart that you are right. I have faith he will live and that God will not call him home." Her face glowed with a light deep within.

❧

Soon, a packet of letters arrived, banded together by the post office. Nettie eagerly sorted them by date and settled back to reading.

> *My dearest Nettie,*
> *Your letter arrived telling of the birth of our son. I say the words over and over to myself and still can't believe they are true. Billy sounds like a fine name. I know you had your father in mind when you named him. Russ and I pray every day for his strength and determination to live. I pray, too, that I might soon be home to see you both. We are on the move again. Marching, always marching. I can't tell you where we are going, only that I hope the next battle will end the war. War is such a hideous thing. I'm sure after I return home the memories I bring along are mine forever. The only good thing to come of being here is the friendships I've made.*

She sat back and folded the pages, trying to envision him reading her letters and the look on his face when he had learned about Billy. There was still much unsettled business between them but the problems looming so large and insurmountable, keeping them distant from each other, were becoming smaller as the months passed. Maybe they were both changing with the winds that crossed the Atlantic.

Nettie stood up and stretched her arms above her head. She was eager to move about again. There was less of a rubbery feeling in her legs as she went to the kitchen to give Billy his feeding. Her new goal became to visit the mill, between feedings of the babies, of course. She felt less antagonism toward Florence, and more pity, especially since she had learned of her demotion. It became equally important to face the young woman again and let her know that she no longer felt intimidated by her.

❧

On May 28, U.S. troops encountered their fist major engagement with the Germans in Cantigny, France. A week later the Americans launched an attack of their own in a remote area called Belleauwood, driving back the Germans in a square mile bastion being held with machine guns. Casualties were heavy on both sides. Jim was one of the first wounded when shrapnel pierced his leg, leaving a deep, jagged tear from knee to ankle. He had cried out in pain. In spite of Derrick's attempt to stem the flow of blood, there was little he could do except stand by and watch as his friend was carried off to the field hospital. In a short time he was transferred to a Red Cross hospital farther behind the lines. Derrick felt the anguish of not knowing where Jim was being sent. His commander was sympathetic but too busy with maneuvers to follow through on finding out Jim's immediate whereabouts.

The regiment marched on toward Paris and a pseudo celebration. Each step of the way Derrick worried about his friend. He often thought of Jim's premonition of not making it through the war. It cut deeply into his heart. Some men's convictions came true on the battlefield. He prayed Jim's was not among them.

Derrick saw nothing of Russ as they marched. With little time to make new friends, his loneliness for his two best pals became acute. All the men were comrades in arms, but there existed little of the give and take of the special friendships bonded between the three men. Mail from home was almost nonexistent adding to Derrick's feeling of isolation. During a rest period while rations were being distributed, the men sat on the hill overlooking a field fertile with rich black loam. As they ate they watched the women planting with their backs bent to the task. When Derrick finished eating he left his pack on the hillside and walked down through the loose soil. He stopped at a matronly woman with a coarse shawl about her shoulders and a scarf tied around her head. She straightened and looked at him suspiciously before a broad smile widened her face as she recognized his uniform.

Derrick scooped up a handful of seeds out of her basket and motioned to the soil. He repeated the gesture several times before she understood.

"Ah," she nodded and bent to the seeds again, showing him her plan of planting.

Row by row they worked their way toward the other end of the huge field. Unnoticed by Derrick, other soldiers came to the aid of the other women who planted the wide expanse. On top of the ridge the regiment commander paused in calling the orders he was obliged to issue. He delayed the move by an hour before his shrill whistle recalled the men to their march.

Derrick straightened his tired back and kissed the woman on the cheek. Her smile and nod of appreciation mingled with her tears. In front of her dirty apron her hands folded in a prayerful attitude as she watched him walk away. Then when he and the other men stood looking down at the planted field, the soldiers raised their arms in a salute and the women answered in unison with a sweeping wave of their hands.

Derrick often wondered why the commander had delayed the march. Long after he had been on the road he saw the women's waving hands and the love that passed from their eyes. There had been no need of a barrier like words. A lump caught in his throat when he remembered. Someday he would tell Nettie and Billy.

❧

French citizens, six deep, lined the Avenue du President Wilson in Paris on July 4, 1918. Derrick permitted his eyes to stray at times to witness the pride on the faces of the French people. No more than himself, he thought, as he stole a brief look at the statue of George Washington as they passed it in the square. They had paraded in other cities on their way to the Front but here they felt the proximity of the Germans. They shared firsthand with the French people the throes of war. The Allies painted a rugged picture of military might affecting all who witnessed the parade. In his mind Derrick saluted for Jim as they passed an arrangement of American bunting. He missed him with a yearning he had not thought possible. There had been little news, only that he was on the mend. He recalled Jim's passion for going to Paris. He would have been so proud to march down the avenue with thousands of onlookers cheering him on. Rumor had been passed along that Jim would be released from the Red Cross hospital and would be rejoining his regiment sometime after the parade. Derrick's heart beat wildly at the prospect.

The parade route ended abruptly and the men fell into lines of march that wound around to the edge of the city. There they met waiting units and immediately were on the move again. When they were out of city limits they were permitted a short rest on the banks of the river. It had been a stirring but tiring day.

Cold rations again, thought Derrick, and he ate only enough to satisfy the hunger pangs he had been feeling ever since the parade. He longed for some of Cook's stew and biscuits. He tried to drive the thought out of his mind but it became an all-consuming obsession. He got up and tossed the half empty tin into the trash receptacle and lay back down on the grass, his hands behind his head. Loneliness filled him. It was getting more and more impossible to put thoughts of home out of his mind. Even while studying the puffy clouds overhead he imagined he was looking up from the spacious lawn in front of the Traum. The sky was the same everywhere. Only when he looked across the water to the quaint barn and the old waterwheel did it bring him back to France.

"That's enough daydreaming for one day, Corporal Homes."

Derrick struggled to stand up and adjust his uniform. He stared at the speaker with the bright light from the sky dimming his eyes. Then he lunged for the soldier. "Jim, you old dog, you." The men embraced in a hearty reunion, then fell to the ground laughing and slapping each other on the back.

"Let me look at you." Derrick held him off as questions tumbled from his mouth. "How are you? When did you get out of the hospital? Did you meet any of those French lassies you're always talking about?"

Jim held up his hands defensively. "Hold on there. The Red Cross nurses were even better than the French women and they could speak English, too," Jim boasted with a wink. "I never made it to the parade though. They didn't want to tax my strength," he said laughing and quickly adding, "so they sent me back to the line."

"How bad was it?" Derrick asked seriously.

"My leg got the worst. After it healed I did special exercises to get it back in shape. You know the story. Patch them up and send them out to do it all over again."

"Don't even think of it. It's a relief to know you have had the injury you were so worried about and now you're as good as new. Now, let's have no more talk about not making it through the war. You were spared for better things," he beamed broadly.

"At least I got some new uniforms. Maybe getting shot up wasn't so bad at all." He ducked as Derrick cuffed him on the ear. They stood up when the whistle blew and the order came for moving out. Neither of them wanted to think about where they were headed. They were just content to be marching side by side again.

Three days later they received word that the Germans waged the greatest battle of the war to date, the Second Battle of Marne. After the news it became apparent that they were headed for a major push through the front lines. Marching was unrelenting with few rest stops and the end of each day found Jim limping. Jim and Derrick had little time for talk as their unit joined others for an unknown destination in a war that seemed like it would never end.

thirteen

Maribel stood over Billy's drawer bed. She jiggled it impatiently. Then she hurried over to inspect Jamie in the serving room off the kitchen. "Jamie isn't fussing as much as he did at the Haven. He must like it here." She flicked her braids over her shoulders and squinted importantly. "Aunt Nettie, Mama said to tell you she would come for Jamie in a few days, after her ailing is better."

"No hurry, dear. I'm sorry to hear your mother is sick. Nothing serious, I hope."

"Her throat is sore when she swallows. Papa gave her some liniment to rub on her chest. She's feeling some better."

"Jamie does seem a bit happier, doesn't he?" Nettie asked as she hugged her niece. "And did you see how Billy is filling out?" Nettie tried hard to smile over the child's announcement, obviously her reason for coming.

"Jamie looks a little better but Billy looks the same to me. Papa says we mustn't be impatient with the little rascals. Early babies are a little slow in the beginning, but they soon catch up."

Nettie laughed at her choice of words. "Your Papa is right, of course."

"There is a new building going up at the Haven," Maribel informed them as Mary combed out one of the child's straggly braids. "The orphans are going to live in it when the state gets them ready." Her lips pursed with the importance of her news. "I sure hope they send some help along or Mama is going to get awful busy." She wagged her head and made a face.

Long after Maribel was gone, Nettie and Mary chuckled over her visit. "What a precocious child. She certainly stays on top of the comings and goings of the Haven. I really miss her. Maribel is like a little mother. She sees to it that all the babies are fed on time, and if you are running a little late with their bottles she stands at your side until you get the job done." Mary laughed heartily then sobered with thought. "She worries over them when they are sick. She's going to be just like her mother, I expect. Speaking of which, I don't wonder why Elise is sick," Mary clucked. "She takes in every abandoned child and stray cat for miles around, always considering her own health last. I wish she'd think of herself sometimes." Mary shook her head.

Nettie nodded. "Lise spoke of taking in children from other counties. That must be what Maribel meant. The child is right, of course. What will she do for help? I have her right arm," she reminded Mary with a sly smile.

Mary blushed. "She always calls me that though I can't imagine I do any more than anyone else at the Haven. There is always someone around to help with the work. They come to the home needing a place to stay, whether they are runaways or just down on their luck. You would wonder how they hear of the place. We must be getting quite a reputation. It fills a need for them and Elise. The help there is appreciated and treated well. They are always so reluctant to leave when the time comes. In fact, I don't think I ever want to leave the Haven. There is so much love there. It's contagious." She smiled with memory.

"Don't say that, Mary. If the right young man comes along there will be no question of staying with Elise," Nettie teased.

"No man wants a woman who is a cripple," Mary snapped. "And I don't want to be an albatross around any man's neck."

"Why, Mary, no one ever thinks of you as a cripple. I admit I noticed your limp when we first me but your goodness far outshines any affliction. You are truly a woman of God. I never realized you harbored such feelings. Why, you were married once. Surely your husband didn't think of you as an albatross." Nettie was flushed with embarrassment.

"No, he never did." Mary stared out of the window. "He treated me like a queen," she remembered softly. "But it was a long time ago and we were young and in love. I learned to accept the legs the good Lord saw fit to give me. My husband was a saint to overlook it, but I expect no other man to do the same." She took Nettie's hands in her own. "Not another word about it." She smiled and changed the subject. "Some of the women go to the Haven to escape the mill. It is said that Tice and his cronies are terrible to work for." She avoided Nettie's curious glance.

"Still? After all my visits? Why didn't Derrick see it," she wondered aloud.

"I can't speak of the present, only the past. I hope your visits did some good so the women who work there are respected as human beings. Elise treats the animals on the farm more kindly, I dare say." Mary's face showed relief when a motorcar stopped in the driveway. She hurried to the door to find Elise standing there. They embraced as though they had not seen each other for a long time. Mary took the basket from her hand and ushered her into the nursery.

Elises arms were bare; a simple loose shift seemed to flow over her thin body. Upswept hair emphasized her long white throat. In spite of her cool appearance, wisps of hair escaped and clung in damp ringlets around her neck. The heat of the summer day was oppressive.

Nettie fanned herself and Jamie with a Japanese fan as he lay in the cradle, clad in nothing but a diaper. A fine rash covered his chest and under the folds of his chin. "You've made a remarkable recovery, Lise. We just heard you were ailing."

"Must have been Maribel telling tales out of school again. That child could be the town crier." They laughed as Mary passed out tall glasses of lemonade. "She also must have told you I was coming to take Jamie home," she added quietly. "She loves to break the news."

"She mentioned it," Nettie answered.

"Let's take a look at him." Elise stared down at the baby in the cradle that Nettie rocked with her foot. "What a change!" she exclaimed, leaning over to have a close look at Jamie. "His eyes are brighter and his color is so good. You are a miracle worker, Mary." She squeezed her hand.

"I had nothing to do with it, Elise," Mary denied. "Look where his gaze goes." She stood back as Elise stared open-mouthed at Nettie.

"You? The last time I was here you wanted no part of Jamie." She sat solidly on a dining room chair.

Nettie remained silent, the corners of her mouth twitching in agitation.

"I don't know how to thank you, Nettie." Elise arranged the covers in the bottom of the basket. "I'm so glad for your change of heart. We have a new nursery for children like him." She stepped forward to pick up the child but Nettie moved in front of her.

"I have no objections to your holding Jamie but I want it clearly understood he is not going home with you." Nettie looked steadily at her sister.

Elise sighed and studied Nettie for along time before she spoke. "These babies won't always be content to stay in their cradles, Nettie dear. When Billy and Jamie are a little older they will be a handful. They are so close in age it will be like having twins. Think about what you are asking, Nettie." She put her arm around her sister's shoulder and together they walked to stand at the window overlooking the fields below.

Elises words were kind and loving. Nettie choked with

emotion as she whispered, "I can get help."

"Mary is here only on loan," Elise reminded her.

"I know." She sent Mary a loving look and reached for her hand. "We will find someone else."

"What do you think Derrick will say?"

"He will say I did the right thing." Nettie held her ground.

"Jamie is a ward of the state. There is much to consider here," Elise argued.

"We can have a lawyer draw up the papers when Derry comes home." A fine bead of perspiration formed on Nettie's upper lip; determination hardened her face. Absently, she tucked wisps of hair into the coil at her neck.

Sister stood her ground against sister. Off to the side Mary waited, her hands twisting the handles of the basket.

"You're taking on a big job, Nettie," Elise argued.

"You took on a much bigger one, Lise."

"I guess I did, didn't I?" She smiled broadly and enfolded Nettie in her arms. "The only thing I ask is for Derrick to help make the final decision. He may not want to share his son with a stranger, you know."

Nettie nodded with a distant look in her eyes. *When Derry comes home it will be such a joyous reunion,* she thought. *If only there weren't so much to set right between us.*

੨੦

Unexpectedly, Nettie stopped in at the mill. She drove the Model-T herself, letting Mary stay home to tend to the babies. Outside on the brick were sprawled painted words, vulgarities about lovers of the Germans, spies, and traitors, accusations casting doubts on and offenses at the Waller family. She reached out to touch the stains of hatred, as though her fingertips could physically remove the words from the bricks. Tears stung her eyes as she mounted the steps to the mill. Her father would be crushed to have his Americanization so deliberately refuted.

When she stepped into the building and heard the hum of machinery and smelled the slightly acrid odor of the silk, it produced a calming effect. She realized how much she missed the visits. From the side of the large room where the machines droned, women called out and waved. Her heart was warmed. They looked happy to see her. Not taking the time for pleasantries, Nettie gathered their warm greetings to her bosom and headed straight for Tice's office.

Tice was holding a meeting with the superintendents. They jumped to their feet when she came blustering into the room and quickly scurried to imaginary duties. Alone, Nettie stood facing Tice across the desk. He looked down at her with light amusement creasing his cheeks.

"Mr. Tice, please ask the janitor to remove those hateful words from the side of the building," she requested.

"Now, now, Mrs. Homes. There is little use because they will only appear again. It is a waste of time and money to take it off. No one bothers about it anymore." He tucked his thumbs in his vest and rocked on his heels.

"*I* see it. *I* am offended for my father and sister and our entire family, but most of all for my husband who fights *against* the Germans. Is there no decency in this world? I don't care if a man has to remove the words every day or cover then up with fresh paint. I want it done." Her eyes blazed and her cheeks were aflame with indignation.

Tice hurried around the desk and pulled a chair behind Nettie. "It shall be done, my dear, make no mistake. They will be removed immediately." He walked into the hall and barked some orders. He came back rubbing his hands. "To what do we owe this unexpected pleasure? By the way, I hear you have a son. Congratulations."

She nodded in acceptance but hurried on. "My visit is unexpected today but in the future they will be even more regular than before. . .my confinement. I hear it said that the women who work here are often dissatisfied. I want to speak to them today and in the future. The Waller name should be equated with a happy, healthy atmosphere. A few changes are necessary."

Tice sat behind his desk and fingered some papers. "The workers are always grumbling about something. . .even when conditions are satisfactory. That is the nature of the beast." He chuckled until his large abdomen rocked slightly.

Nettie ignored his attempt at humor. "And how are you doing in service to the Lord, Mr. Tice?" Nettie stared guilelessly across the desk.

"I try to give the task an hour now and again." He avoided her unrelenting gaze. "I must confess we are extremely overworked in the mill, trying to anticipate the holiday rush. Our busy season, you know."

"You made me a promise, Mr. Tice," Nettie reminded him.

"And I am a completely devoted husband. And Florence. . . Miss Higgins never crosses this threshold," he assured her. "May I inquire to your health and the baby's, and what do you hear from Mr. Homes?" Sweat poured from his brow.

Nettie realized she was going to receive no more assurance on the promise. "We are all fine. I'll see you in a few days, Mr. Tice. Now I must talk to the women."

"But the heat upstairs is oppressive if you are not used to it, my dear," he cautioned as he hurried around to open the door.

Nettie considered his warning as she climbed to the second floor of the factory. When she opened the door of the main room she was overcome by a blast of heat she had not expected. It took her breath away and she gasped for air. She nearly staggered into the department. Women tended the rows of machinery in sweat-drenched, skimpy dresses. A few raised their arms lethargically; others stared past her as though they hardly knew her. Slowly she walked the length of the department and went immediately down the stairs at the far end. For a long time she stood in the small hallway regaining her composure before she stepped into the first floor where the operators were cool by comparison. There, the workers were more jovial and she tried to draw them out about working conditions. Most of them eyed her suspiciously and offered no ammunition for her cause. At the end of the row, resetting her downed loom, Florence Higgins turned her back when she saw Nettie approach.

"How are you today, Florence?" Nettie waited until the woman finally faced her.

"As good as can be expected, Hettie."

"My first name is Nettie. If you are going to use it, please get it right," Nettie retorted stiffly.

"Oh, I thought Derrick called you Hettie." There was mocking in her eyes. "I can't wait for Derrick to get home. I. . .we all miss him so."

"Will you call a meeting of the women who work here? For some reason I think they might listen to you. We can meet in the church to discuss ways of improving working conditions in the factory. Please, Florence. Can I count on you?" Nettie held out her hand and watched the woman flinch slightly before she took it.

"Okay, okay. We might be interested in what you have to say, Hettie."

"And one thing more," Nettie answered through measured words. "Please don't call me Hettie again, or Mr. Homes, Derrick." She walked out into the fresh air and fanned her collar around her face. Her visit after months of absence made her feel like a stranger to women she once thought of as friends. Even Pamela, upstairs in that terrible heat, only gave her a glance. Now she chose to rely on Florence Higgins to gather in the fold. She must be mad, she told Mary when she arrived home. Only a mad woman would call on her enemies to carry out her plan.

fourteen

The war intensified. American and German prisoners were many; the number of wounded and dead on both sides was staggering. While Derrick and Jim rested behind the line, a tent was set up to provide the men with their first hot food in weeks. After a hearty meal of stew and biscuits Derrick over-heard a sergeant and lieutenant discussing the plan of march for the company's new assignment. The destination was the Argonne Forest. Outside in the cool air Derrick closed his eyes and sank to his haunches. He felt the rough stake of the mess tent against his back. He did not move.

Jim came hurrying around the front of the tent, toppling Derrick as he rounded the corner. He grabbed Derrick by the arm and helped him up. Through clenched teeth he whispered, "I just heard. I hoped it was just a rumor but I can see by your face it isn't. I think we better find Russ."

The march was scheduled to begin at daylight. Word had been passed along the line that this was the main thrust. The German's were offensive players to this point and they were largely successful. But wars were not won by remaining on the defensive. The men knew it and dreaded what it meant. One of their divisions had scored a victory in a counter offensive at Belleauwood. The time had come to do more than hold the line.

The men were unusually subdued as they waited in their tents in the darkness for the appointed hour. With certainty this long march would culminate in a decisive battle. With

equal certainty it would take it's toll. With the aid of camou-
flaged flashlights they wrote hasty letters home and packed
their few belongings. Emotions were grim; words were few.

Russ wriggled into his friends' small tent long after taps.
He lay on the ground between their cots, a luxury they had
not been afforded on the Front. At times the sky lit with the
shelling miles away and they could see the outline of his
arms clasped behind his head. His thin face drew into exaggerated lines as he spoke of their long weeks of separation.

"I heard you wanted to see me. Many men do this night.
It's been a while since I made my rounds." He reached out
and grasped both their hands. "Stay well, boys, stay well," he
said huskily.

"Pray with us, Chaplain," Jim always called him formally
when he was deeply troubled. "I know my time is coming. I
feel so helpless. There is so much to do. . .to say."

Russ sat up, staring at him through the dark night. "Jim,
don't be afraid. The Lord Jesus Christ is with you as you
march into this battle." He took Jim's hands and together
they knelt in prayer between the cots.

"Derrick, I'm concerned about you. From the day I met
you I knew you were different. Jim tells me so much about
himself but you are a very private person. I respect that. I
worry about it, too. What can I do for you, lad?"

Derrick faced him blindly on the hard ground. "I want to
pray with you and Jim," he said thickly. "I know the time for
confession has come." He bowed his head and quietly admitted, "I am a cringing coward, more than any man here. I want
to cry and tear my clothes. I want to bolt and run. Help me,
Russ. I am so ashamed."

"You have already proved yourself to be anything but a
coward, Derrick. I know you are afraid. Every man here

dreads the Argonne. We have all heard of the bloody battles that rage there. Let's ask His blessings on ourselves and our comrades. None of us knows what tomorrow may bring. Just because I carry the cross doesn't make me bulletproof. I confess I have the same sense of dread, not only for myself, but for all of you. Let our fears be tempered with His love and promise."

When Russ slipped quietly out of the tent, the call of "Chaplain" came from all sides, from sleepless soldiers who waited in the darkness for a comforting word.

Reveille came brazenly in the early morning hours, just after sleep had come to many. At the first blaring notes, Jim and Derrick scrambled to their feet and pulled on their boots. Coats were quickly buttoned and morning rituals dispensed of. In the darkness, with the help of dim kerosene lanterns. they mustered in the fields near the tents. No one spoke. Formation was orderly and practiced. By the time the dismal gray light of dawn glared on the horizon the men were on their way, marching down country lanes, across fields and rough terrain, in as straight a line as possible, to join other troops headed for the Argonne.

Derrick and Jim were together as always but they separated briefly when rations were dispensed and diagrams of the battlefield were laid out to small groups of men. After the briefing Derrick kept a diligent account of Jim's whereabouts. He recognized the look of relief on Jim's face when they made eye contact. He also witnessed the grim determination marching with him. Others had the presence, too, a resignation; in some it was a look of finality. He saw Jim hurrying to some unknown destination. Derrick knew his own face registered his dread, his acceptance of the inevitable. On the second day of march Derrick sensed a change in Jim. His agitation eased and his eyes shone with a new light. Derrick became more concerned than ever.

"He's here, Derrick. I know He's marching with me now. I feel His love. I hope He knows mine."

"Jesus knows what all of us are feeling, Jim." There was no question in his mind of what he was talking about. Derrick tried to take Jim's focus off of himself. "We all feel His protection going into battle, Jim. I keep telling you, you have had your share of injuries. Everything will be okay." Abruptly he turned the subject to himself. "I never asked you, friend, but if I don't make it, tell Nettie I love her. Tell her that. . .I found Jesus. She'll be glad to know it." Derrick broke off as a round of machine gun fire flattened them to the ground.

From their position at the top of the knoll Jim smiled sadly. "You do the same for me and Josephine, hear?"

"I won't have to. I'm going to be the best man at your wedding, remember?"

Derrick tried to laugh but the sound was more choking than humorous.

"Yeah, yeah. Someday we'll be sitting around telling war stories, I know."

The heavy fire kept them pinned to the ground. Hand grenades spattered puffs of smoke and flame across the terrain. A grenade landed close to Derrick and Jim. They dove into a shallow ravine. Overhead a hail of bullets told them the Germans knew their position. They scrambled sideways in the mud to put distance between them. A few seconds of quiet made Derrick believe that they had escaped the barrage but in the short moment of relief, something flew through the air and landed near his right leg. In the same instant, Jim leaped from a thicket of cover and threw himself on top of the grenade. Derrick screamed words of denial. Around him fire burst into smothering smoke. When the air cleared he knew Jim had made the supreme sacrifice. Derrick cried out in anger and despair. Pain coursed through his mind and, more excruciatingly, through his body. Then all was blackness.

ॐ

Nettie stood before the fifty-five women who worked in the mill. The inside of the church felt cool even in the afternoon heat. She wondered how Florence had convinced them to come to the meeting. They were a surly looking group of women who sat before her in their working clothes. When she greeted them, many by name, she soon discovered the casual friendliness that had brought them together in the mill no longer applied to the meeting room. She felt their detachment, their suspicions, and, in some cases, their fear for even attending the meeting. As the women settled in and talked among themselves, it became apparent to Nettie from the tone of their voices that they expected her to produce results once they openly vented their grievances. She wiped her brow, dreading the confrontations with Mr. Tice. She took a big breath and remembered her commitment to these young women.

Nettie rapped for attention as voices raised heatedly. "I want to help each and every one of you, honestly, I do. Reform won't come all at once. Please, help me, won't you?"

She held out her arms to them. Sullen stares waited for her to continue. "Thank you. And I most heartedly thank you for coming today. I've heard some of your problems. Now I want you to form little groups and decide which grievance is the most pressing."

"We're not here for a Sunday school class, Nettie." Florence Higgins, who appointed herself spokeswoman for the group, rose from her seat and pointed her finger at her. "I got them here, now you deliver on your promise. Who owns the mill, you or Tice?"

Nettie blushed uncomfortably. "The ownership of the silk mill is not the problem here," Nettie retorted, keeping Florence in her gaze. "We must work together for reform. I plan to meet with Mr. Tice in the morning. Right now I want you to name the first thing on your mind when it comes to improved conditions. That will be the starting point. Please trust me. I won't let you down. I promise." Nettie stepped down from the podium and directed the women into small groups. When they were all seated, she led Florence to the far end of the room.

"You are to be my right arm, Florence." Inwardly she shuddered at her own choice of words. "When each group has decided on a grievance, I want you to gather them on a paper and tell me the most popular. That is where we begin." She tried to ignore the flashing green eyes glaring up at her. *Oh, Lord*, she prayed, *help me to do the right thing.* Then Nettie took a seat in the back of the room. She waited while Florence polled the women.

Together she and Florence walked to the front of the room. Nettie smiled nervously as she began to hush the crowd. "Tomorrow morning I shall meet with Mr. Tice and form a plan to give each of you a ten-minute break from your machines, both in the morning and in the afternoon. Be patient, please. It may not happen overnight. Let's agree to meet here once a month to air your complaints. . .and our progress. It won't be easy but together we can do it." As Nettie collected her notebook and purse, a loud round of applause came from the women. Their once-suspicious faces now cheered her on. A great sense of relief and pride came over her.

Early the next morning Nettie announced her presence in the factory. On her way into the building she noticed that the outside walls had been cleared of the hate slurs. She planned first to compliment Mr. Tice on his attention to the matter. It would help to start out with a compliment, she reasoned. Quiet waves of encouragement greeted her from the women at the machines when she passed through the first floor of the mill.

Tice pored over a set of ledgers as she stood waiting. When he glanced up he took out his pocket watch and squinted. "You're early," he mumbled irritably.

"Pardon me," she answered just as irritably.

"You never show up until ten o'clock, What's on your mind this time? You must think it's important." Tice picked his teeth, making no effort to rise in her presence.

"Mr. Tice," she drew herself up to full height, "may I remind you I am part owner of this factory. What right do you have to question my visits?" Tears stung her eyes but she fought them back.

"Mrs. Homes, your husband and I reached an agreement. He didn't interfere with me and I didn't interfere with him. I liked the arrangement much better before you took his place. Now, if you don't mind, I have more pressing matters than to hold your hand and tell you what your visits mean to these darling girls," he said with sarcasm. "You have met all of them, one by one, and you gave each one of them a little Christmas present. Now, why don't you run along home? I expect your husband will be back in a few months. I can handle this until then." He gave her a broad wink and ushered her to the door.

Nettie refused to be seen out. She lowered her head, took a big breath to remind herself of her mission, slammed the door, and marched back to stand in front of his desk. "For one who was caught in such an embarrassing position a few months ago, you certainly have recovered."

"Oh, that little flirtation? My wife knew about it. It seems she has tolerated my shenanigans for years. I did some community service, more for your benefit than mine, but that's where it ends."

"Not quite." Nettie removed her gloves slowly and sat in the chair facing Tice. "It seems we have a few problems needing attention."

"I heard all about your little meeting with the girls. It won't work. They've tried to organize against me before."

"These women aren't against you, Mr. Tice. They simply want better working conditions. Their health and well-being depends on it. I don't want this factory to be one of those sweatshops you hear about in New York. We have always cared about our people. I remember my father working side by side with them during a heavy load. They matter a great deal to me and my sister, Mr. Tice."

His raucous laughter echoed down the hall. "If they don't want to work here there are plenty of girls waiting in the streets who would be glad for any job they can get." He tried to stare her down.

Nettie shook inside, hoping her trembling was not visible. She argued long and hard but still he would not budge. "Perhaps you would like to be relieved of your position," she said at last resort.

Tice walked to a small safe behind his desk and produced a piece of paper that he held under her nose. "Your father gave me an ironclad agreement of service for as long as I want it. Besides, what would you do without my expertise, Mrs. Homes? There is no one who could keep the operation running here. You need me," he reminded her.

She sat back deflated but she argued firmly, "I believe it is time for a change."

"What do you propose?" he asked as he sat on the edge of the desk. "I must say, you have your father's gumption, Mrs. Homes. I thought you would have left a long time ago."

Fresh air fanned her flaming cheeks; Nettie leaned forward. "The workers need a break, midmorning and midafternoon. It is hard work with five long hours before and after lunch."

"How long?" he snapped.

"Ten minutes."

"Ten minutes, twice a day? Do you know how much that is going to cost?"

"It will cost less than if they work without a rest," she argued.

"No!" he slammed his fist on the desk.

"Fine. Tomorrow. . .early. . .I will come by with a lawyer to read your agreement."

"All right, we can try it for a week, but if there is any loss of production there will be no more breaks, do you understand?"

Nettie got up on shaky legs. She extended her hand over the desk. "I think we understand each other perfectly, Mr. Tice. I'll tell the women. They will be delighted."

All the way home she could hardly contain herself. *Oh, Derry will be so proud of me. The women even cheered!* She was so happy.

When she arrived at the Traum, Nettie could hear Jamie's angry protests at having had to wait for his feeding. On the way to the nursery she nearly ran headlong into Randall Homes as he stepped out of the parlor and directly into her path.

"Papa Homes, how good to see you." She stepped back and stared at his drooping mouth. "What is it? Has something happened to Derry?" Her hands flew to her lips. Her face blanched. "Is he. . . ?"

Randall took her hands and smiled weakly. "No, Nettie everything is fine except for Jamie who has been waiting impatiently for you. See to him first. Then we can talk. I'll wait in the parlor." He winked and smiled indulgently, twirling his hat in his hand.

Jamie nursed hungrily. While she gazed down into his large brown eyes, Nettie tried to push the feeling of impending doom from her mind. She willed the child to sleep with his feeding. Finally, Mary came and put him in the cradle.

"What do you know, Mary," Nettie demanded.

"I only know Papa Homes is nervous. . .upset. That's all. He wouldn't tell me. He paced the room long before you returned home." She answered quietly so as not be overheard. Her face mirrored Nettie's concern.

"Come with me, please." The fear in Nettie's eyes gave a new depth to their color. Arm in arm they walked into the parlor. Randall stood by the window, white knuckles pressed on the drum table at his side. He turned slowly when he heard them behind him.

"Papa." Nettie held out her hand as she looked up at him. Her wide questioning eyes never left his.

"Sit down, both of you."

Mary clasped Nettie's arm and led her to the settee.

"I have intercepted two letters at the post office. The postmaster is a friend who I alerted to be on the lookout—"

"Derry is dead," Nettie sobbed.

"No, my dear. He is wounded but alive."

Her head snapped up and she was on her feet, wringing her

hands. "Tell me. Tell me. Where are the letters? How is he? Oh, God, help him," she cried.

Randall remained seated as Mary tried to calm her. "The first is from the War Department. It tells us he was wounded in action and is being treated in a Red Cross hospital in a place called Fleury-sur-Aire. When he recovers he is to be sent home with decorations. It seems he and another man are receiving medals for heroism."

"And the other letter. Is it from Derrick?"

"No, it is from a man named Chaplain Russell Parks."

Mary gasped and hugged Nettie to her. "May we read it?" she choked the words. Together she and Nettie sat on the settee while Mary read aloud the short note from Russell.

They are both heroes. One man, Jim Rawley, made the supreme sacrifice in order to save Derrick. Realizing he knew his God just before he was called to heaven doesn't completely comfort the personal loss that Derrick and I are feeling but we are trying to get through our grief. I visited Derrick in the field hospital he was taken to just after his injury, in the ruins of a church in Neuvilly not far from the battleground. The wounds he sustained were to his chest and right leg. Casualties were extremely heavy. Please, rest assured, Derrick will make a complete recovery. He needs time to heal the wounds of spirit and body. His healing is in God's hands.

Your servant in Christ,
Russell Parks, Chaplain

The women wept together in each other's arms. Then Mary insisted Randall sit beside Nettie. He took her in his arms and tried to console her convulsing sobs. Once she paused and looked at him, tears sparkling on her long lashes. "Just a few minutes ago I hurried home, feeling so elated. I wanted to tell Derry how proud he will be of me because I championed the mill workers' request for a break from their work." She cried into Randall's large handkerchief. "It seems so insignificant now."

"Hush, my child. It *is* important and Derrick *will* be proud of you as we are of him. Hold on to these little triumphs and care for the babies. They need you. Soon Derrick will be home and your lives, back in order. I am going to stop at the parsonage to arrange a prayer service for Derrick and for Jim's family, and for all the brave men who fight for us. Oh, to have him home again." He wiped his eyes.

Long after Randall left the Traum, Nettie stayed in the parlor. When it grew dark, Mary lit a lamp and hovered about her in despair. At feeding time she wordlessly brought Jamie to her. In the evening when the house was quiet, Mary finally helped her to bed. They prayed together and wept together. Nettie and Mary were also grateful to a man named Russell Parks who had paused from his many duties to write home about Derrick.

fifteen

"I've heard rumors that negotiations for peace talks are underway. It's no secret the Germans are on the run. I pray this war will soon be over and everyone can get their lives back in order." Russ sat by Derrick's bed flexing his fingers against each other. All through the hospital ward beds were crammed into every possible cranny with little room for bedside tables or medicine carts. Wounded men lined the walls, others walked the halls. Here and there bandaged soldiers asked for water or cried out with the pain of traction or recent surgery. Salvation Army volunteers dispensed gifts of toiletries and wrote letters for those unable to do so.

"You must mean those who have lives to put back in order," Derrick said bitterly. His chest was still heavily bandaged and a small drainage tube ran to a bottle under his bed. His right leg, in a thick cast, was held at an angle by a contraption above the bed. He grimaced with pain when Russ tried to help him into a more comfortable position.

"I miss him almost as much as you do. I didn't get to see him every day but he became a very special friend to me, too. Jim wouldn't want us to grieve for him, Derrick. Try to remember the good he did in his life. Remember the warmth and charm, that head-on approach to life that was with him until the end. There is great solace for me in his acceptance of the Lord. He expected to be called, you know. Thank God he did so with a pure heart. I am so overjoyed he found Jesus. Foremost in his life, he treasured your friendship. He certainly proved his devotion beyond the shadow of a doubt. 'Greater love hath no man than this, that a man lay down his life for his friends.' " As Russ quoted from John 15:13, tears streamed down his cheeks but a look of peace emanated from his eyes.

"I've thought of that passage a thousand times lying here in this bed. When someone saves your life you owe him yours. How can I ever repay my life for his? Oh, God," Derrick sobbed, more readily in his injured condition.

"He wouldn't expect your physical life, Derrick. Remember him by keeping your spiritual life for Christ. That's what Jim would want."

"Maybe Jim was the lucky one. At least he won't have to go home a cripple." Derrick's face flushed with anger and frustration.

Russ shook his head emphatically. "I heard what the doctors told you. A little limp is not a bad price to pay for your life, Derrick. I can't believe you think Jim is better off than you. A new son waits at home to meet his father as well as a beautiful wife who loves you." The strain of being surrounded by pain and suffering sagged Russ's shoulders and creased tired lines into his face.

"Oh, don't sit and hold my hand, Russ. I can be miserable by myself. I need only to look around me or to read the casualty list every day. Why don't you go to someone who needs you?"

"You need me right now Derrick, and *I* need you. Do you think that just because I am a man of the cloth that I have no need of comfort or friendships? That I don't have questions and doubts? I need you more than you think."

Derrick studied Russ's wizened face intently. He squeezed his eyes tightly shut and clenched his jaw. He felt his pain. Then, wordlessly, he stretched out his hand to Russ. It was quickly grasped and held through a moment of shared mourning.

Russ paused a long moment before he wiped his eyes and

cleared his throat before he began to speak. "I made a special trip to see you today." He took a letter from his pocket and held it up. "You see *I* am getting the mail now." He smiled and clicked his tongue. "Aren't you the least bit curious?" Laugh lines brightened his face.

Derrick made a swipe at the letter but Russ held it far enough away to be out of reach.

"This one's for me. It's from Mary, but I understand one is on the way from Nettie. I wrote to Mary and your wife when you were wounded. I told them about Jim, too."

"What did you say about me?" Derrick demanded to know.

"I told them you sustained a chest and leg wound and would be as good as new with time. I told them that as soon as you could you would write yourself. Did you write yet, Derrick, and if not, why not?"

"I didn't want to tell my wife she would be living with a cripple. I want to give her a way out of a hapless situation when I see her in person. Having Mary around is seeing enough of a cripple."

Russ's eyes widened. He digested Derrick's words slowly. "You never told me Mary had. . .an affliction."

"You never asked. Besides, it doesn't keep her from doing anything."

"Oh?"

It was Derrick's time to remain silent.

"I want you to think about what you just said, Derrick. And there's something else. There are two thoughts I want to leave with you. I may not get back to see you again until the Armistice is signed."

"Go ahead. I've known you long enough to realize you never leave anything unsaid. Out with it, Chaplain Parks." His brooding eyes told Russ he was not joking this time.

The call came for lights out in the ward and visitors around them, mostly other wounded men and volunteers, bid hasty goodbyes. Russ stood up and grasped Derrick's hand. "I want permission to go home to Schiffley with you. I'd like to meet this Mary you told me so much. . .and so little about. I have to thank her personally for easing my time over here by writing to me. The second request—"

The overhead lights blinked their signal and went out immediately, leaving only a glow from a nearby nurses' station. Russ spoke with urgency. "I want to visit Jim's mother and sister in Philadelphia. He asked both of us to do that for him. I figure we owe him much more but what else can we do besides talk to the ones he loved so dearly? What do you say? I can put in a request to accompany you home if you'd like. Think it over, Derrick. Pray about it."

In the semidarkness, Derrick answered thickly, "There's nothing to think over, Russ. I would be honored to have you in my home, to meet Nettie and Mary and my father. Yes, oh, yes," he choked, "we must talk to Jim's family but I didn't know if I would have the courage to see them face to face. With your help I can do it. Thank you, my friend."

Russ grasped Derrick's hand then made his way toward the light in the corridor. On his way he collided with a metal stand. He chuckled and rubbed his shin. Derrick heard his laughter as he walked down the hall.

Russ was right; Derrick thought over his visit as he lay in the darkness. In their shared grief they needed each other. War left only an empty ache. It destroyed so much that was good, homes and land, most of all, lives. If there were any shining deeds to come out of it, it was to be thrown together with men like Jim and Russ and, above all else, to learn the love of God. As he stared at the vague shapes and shadows of the hospital room, hearing the sounds of suffering all around him, he wanted desperately for it all to be over. Maybe Russ was right. They needed time to heal, to get their lives back in order, to put the pain behind them. The news was encouraging. The Germans were on the run. The Americans were breaking through the lines. He had to admit to a certain pride in having helped to make the difference. He prayed that the truce would be called while men like Russ were still alive.

The last person he thought of each night and the first each morning lingered with him this endless time. Now, more than ever he longed to take Nettie in his arms again and feel the comfort of her love. The memory of her face dimmed in his mind. Panic filled the darkness. He could not see her picture on the small table by his bed. Every day he had tried to memorize the details of her beautiful eyes or her pert nose or her wonderful sensitive lips. He wondered how she would welcome him home, if at all, with so many unanswered questions between them. The rifts of the past no longer held importance for him. He could not even remember what they were. If only it was the same for her. Perhaps the crosswinds Nettie wrote about early on were but puffs of vapor on the horizon and had dissipated with the changing currents. In his dreams of home, Derrick saw himself as a new man who, for the first time, was comfortable with himself. He envisioned Nettie as the beautiful young woman she was. Now he remembered her in vivid detail.

&

The tiresome sessions with Mr. Tice were not always victorious but Nettie held on to the feeling of accomplishment. The work breaks were granted and they were successful. Even Tice could not dispute the productiveness of the employees a full month later. He never fully realized just how much the breaks meant to the workers. The first reform was accepted. It brought other measures, like better rest room facilities with sinks for washing, and a real lunch room instead of having to eat hovering behind the moving machines.

The meetings with the women, which began on a monthly

basis, were now held every two weeks with Florence Higgins presiding when Nettie became too pressed for time. The workers discussed the need for a better quality of silk, free from lumps and imperfections that irritated the weavers and frequently shut down the machinery. The women also asked for fans in the summer, especially for the second floor of the factory, where temperatures often reached 118 degrees, when they could not breathe and often passed out with heat exhaustion. In spite of their open forums where many complaints were aired, the ultimate discussion and limited success with Tice belonged to Nettie.

She sat across from him now, studying the dreary office wallpaper dating back to her father's time, while Tice made a point of keeping her waiting by flipping through some invoices. Some things never changed. Henry Tice still insisted on exacting his price for any concessions he agreed to. He always let it be known he was in charge of making money for the Waller sisters and that anything else was secondary. He was often able to back Nettie down from proposing costly improvements. She could not deny some dependence of herself and Elise on the income from the mill. Improvements were often tempered by heated discussions and, ultimately, practicality. While Nettie wanted to run with the workers, at times she was forced to give in to Tice.

"What is it this time, Mrs. Homes?" the edge in his voice betrayed his hostility. He never looked up from reading the papers.

"I think it's high time we did something for you, Mr. Tice. It must be very tedious coming into this depressing place every day and seeing the same dusty bookshelves and worn out furniture."

A moment of enlightenment shone in his eyes. He held out his hands in protest. "I *like* dusty books and old furniture. It makes me feel at home."

"Nevertheless, you should see an improvement in your working conditions, also." She walked slowly about the room, feeling the time-worn, dusty draperies that made her sneeze.

"Mrs. Homes, you never set foot in this office that it doesn't dip into the profits," he argued.

"May I remind you the rest periods didn't reduce the profit by one cent. The lunch room was an unused storage space and the furniture, a donation from a businessman. The only cost so far includes two new sinks and a little plumbing. You approved the facility yourself."

He held his head. "When do you propose to begin work in my office?" he asked sourly.

"The painting can be done at night by the janitor. My dressmaker can make the draperies." She walked excitedly about the room, holding up swatches of material she had tucked in her purse.

Tice moaned with the realization that he was defeated from the moment she had walked in the door. "What do you hear from Mr. Homes?" he asked to distract her.

"He is on his way home, Mr. Tice." She smiled broadly. "With the Armistice practically signed they are sending him home with a dear friend. In a matter of weeks he should be here. Isn't it wonderful?" Nettie's large, blue eyes glowed with a faraway stare. For the first time in months she had high color in her cheeks. She painted a beautiful picture.

Nettie quickly came back to the present and took her chair facing him. "Oh, Mr. Tice, I hear from the majority of the women that they would like to be paid a Christmas holiday."

Immediately he jumped out of his chair, thrashing his arms about and pacing the small room. "You have gone too far this time!" he shouted so loudly Nettie cringed in her seat.

She held her position. "It is said in business circles that we are setting a trend for the betterment of our employees.

Other factories are beginning to copy our example. Doesn't is make you proud, Mr. Tice?"

He pointed to the door. "I will not be manipulated any further. Fix up the office, if you must, but leave the working hours alone, Mrs. Homes, or there will be problems greater than you imagined. Please, leave while I still possess my sanity."

Nettie walked to the door. "Thank you for your time, Mr. Tice. You were most helpful. I'm sure you will admire the office when it is finished." She smiled sweetly as she stood in the hall, collecting her thoughts. Perhaps it was too soon to expect a dramatic change like a holiday. Maybe a little Christmas bonus would appease both sides. She would think on it. She would never admit to Tice it was not the women's idea but her own. There was time for a trend-setting company to make changes. She felt a glow of satisfaction.

Her heart beat wildly in her chest when she thought of Derry coming home soon. God help her to make it right between them. She smiled at the prospect of introducing little Billy to his father. He had grown and filled out in the seven months since he was born. The most distressing thought about the homecoming was telling Derry about Jamie. She tried to put it out of her mind.

"Nettie," Florence called from a small office just off Tice's. "I want to thank you for going to the old man for us. The women are much happier coming to work in the morning, I can tell you. They want me to thank you, too."

"I'm so glad, Florence. These changes are long overdue." An uneasiness still ran between them whenever they came together.

"Nettie, I suddenly realized you have become a. . .friend to me. I'm sorry for. . ."

Nettie waited in silence, not knowing quite how to respond.

"I'm so glad to hear Mr. Homes is all right. I know how

worried you were. I never meant to be. . .All those dreadful things I said. . .Please, forgive me."

Nettie drew a deep breath. "Florence, there is something I must know. Did you see Mr. Homes off when he left the station for the war?"

Her expressive eyes were downcast. She shook her head. "I went to see the soldiers off. I waved to him. . .and to all the boys getting on the train. I went there most of all because of Jack, my friend."

"Thank you for telling me. I know you didn't have to." Nettie put her arm around the taller woman's waist as they walked to the exit. "I suddenly realize I made a friend, too."

"You must have hated me and you were right to be angry. I was jealous. I never thought people in mansions cared about us working girls and I wanted to hurt you. But then I saw how much you wanted to help us. I am engaged to marry one of the boys who went overseas with Mr. Homes. I don't have a ring. We couldn't afford one. Will you come to the wedding when Jack gets back?" Her face lit up with pride. "Jack made it through the war. I'm so happy he did. Mr. Homes, too."

"We'll be delighted to come. Of course, I have to talk it over with my husband." Nettie remembered the dances and late-night parties. Perhaps there would still be social events when she and Derrick settled into a normal family lifestyle but it would be a much fuller and more meaningful life. She bubbled in anticipation. He was coming home.

ॐ

When Derrick and Russ boarded the train in Philadelphia they were silent as the train carried them to Schiffley. They were each intent on their own thoughts. The three women had huddled together in the small parlor as the chaplain told them of Jim's faith and sacrifice. They heard from Russ and Derrick how friendships had been forged and promises made for messages and commitment. Amid their tears and weeping, the three women seemed bonded by a love that would have made Jim proud.

"I'm so glad we took the time," Derrick said with a voice steeped with emotion.

Russ nodded. "I know how anxious you are to get home to your family. It would have been easy to change trains without making the stop. I'll always be glad we did."

Derrick took a deep breath. "Jim would have been glad we did, too. He would have made the effort for us if the situation were reversed. As far as going home, I'm anxious and a little scared."

"You're on the mend, Derrick. Your limp is only slight now. Surely you don't expect Nettie to throw you out of the house over a limp?" Russ chuckled at the prospect.

"I wasn't even thinking of something as simple as a limp. We had some misunderstandings when I left. I never even told her I was drafted. She believed I deserted her." Derrick's voice trailed off uncomfortably. "There are a lot of fences to mend, Russ. I don't know what to expect."

"You never told me."

"I never told anyone except Jim and that was in a weak moment. I'm not proud of it."

"Why is it we make life so complicated?"

Derrick laughed in spite of the gravity of his confession. "What about you? You still want to meet Mary after you learned she is crippled. Why do you want to complicate your own life?"

"In the letters she sent me at the Front, I learned to know Mary by her heart. Perhaps I won't see her affliction. You said so yourself. It doesn't keep her from doing anything she sets her mind to. Some of us have afflictions we can't see but they are there just the same." He leaned his head against the hard cushion of the seat. "I know more about Mary than she may know about herself." He was still grinning when their station was called. They gathered their meager possessions and prepared to begin their lives as civilians.

On the platform Derrick stood listening to the quiet sounds, the late-evening noises of normalcy. If he sensed his friend's impatience to be off, Derrick remained in place, stubbornly listening to the sounds and smelling the fresh cool air. He took his watch from his pocket and checked the time against the station clock he could see through the window of the ticket booth. He turned and stared at the departing train as it disappeared down the long track. He closed his eyes and blinked back the wetness that came with being home again. Then he picked up the small bag containing the only possessions he had salvaged over the past thirteen months, and turned in the direction of the Traum. The time for wondering how Nettie would accept him was past. He was going home to make peace with his wife and to meet his son.

sixteen

"Pamela, Pamela," Nettie called from her car as the young woman came down the steps of the factory at quitting time.

Pamela turned and glanced behind her and looked again at Nettie. She pointed to herself questioningly.

Nettie opened the door and indicated the seat beside her. "Yes, don't be so surprised. Won't you join me? I've been wanting to ask a favor of you. Come sit in the motorcar while we talk."

"Oh, Mrs. Homes. . .Nettie. It's been a long, hard day. You will need a lot of lilac water to sit next to me," she laughed self-consciously.

"Nonsense. Now sit down. We can't have a very good conversation with you hanging on the running board, can we?"

"No, ma'am."

"First I should explain what brings me to ask this favor of you."

"I can't imagine what you could want from me," she commented while checking her dirty fingernails. "I'm just a hard-working girl, you know."

"Exactly. I've seen your dedication. I've also seen the calm manner in which you handle difficult situations when your loom breaks down or when the silks are tedious or, I might add, in dealing with Florence. I know *that* can't always be easy. You handle yourself very well, Pamela."

"Thank you, ma'am."

"Mr. Homes is due to return any day." Nettie tried to contain her voice. "My companion for the past year or more has been a woman who was loaned to me by my sister, Elise, at

158

Valley Haven." She sighed. "The agreement is for her to return to the Haven when Mr. Homes comes back and I no longer need her help. I find I will need extra help even when my husband returns because I want to continue my work at the mill. I've grown so attached to the women." She raised a gloved hand to her brow. "Oh, dear. I'm saying it badly. This needs to be cleared with my husband, of course, but I expect I will need a nanny. Will you possibly consider coming to work for me? I know it would mean leaving a fine job as a weaver. I would arrange for an equal salary, of course. Just tell me if you would consider it, Pamela. I don't expect you to make a rash decision this moment."

"No," she answered firmly.

"No?" Nettie fanned her face. "Oh, dear. Now I must go looking elsewhere."

Pamela sat with her hands over her eyes and mouth. When she looked up at Nettie her face was flushed and wet. "No, I meant I wouldn't need to consider it. Yes, I would love to come to the Traum and be your nanny. It would be an honor."

Nettie let out a shriek and put her arms around Pamela. "I hope you will never be sorry. I am so thrilled you said yes. There is one thing I must ask you."

"Anything."

"This must be our secret until I seal the agreement with Mr. Homes." She tried to still the wild beating of her heart when she thought of the scene to come with Derry. On one hand she was delirious with the thought of having him home again. On the other, she was filled with such a dread at the prospect of airing their problems. "I would offer to drive you home but I must talk to Mr. Tice. Is he still in his office?"

"There was a light on when I passed by. I think I came out last. I stayed to clean some lint out of the machine. He always locks up after were all out." She whispered, "I think he checks up on us."

Nettie mounted the steps of the factory as Pamela walked home on a cloud of anticipation. She walked through the rows of idled looms toward the lighted office. Tice sat behind his desk in his shirt sleeves, a cup of coffee at one elbow and a ledger opened in front of him. Her feet glided noiselessly across the scrolled carpeting. At last he sensed her presence and looked up.

"Don't get up, Mr. Tice. I know it's late but I need to talk with you. Something has been bothering me for a long time."

"Sit down, Nettie."

His unaccustomed use of her Christian name put an element of doubt in her mind that she could state her reason for coming.

He continued to sip his coffee quietly, deliberately. "Nothing has ever tied your tongue before. What is it?"

She sighed deeply and plunged in. "While I pored over the books, I noted a month each year where the figures didn't compare to the other months."

"Oh?"

"I think you know exactly what I mean."

"I made a promise long ago not to divulge this information."

"Mr. Tice, may I remind you that your first obligation is to Elise and me."

"I made a promise and I only revealed it to another soul under an oath of secrecy." He perspired heavily in the cool office.

"Would that have been Mr. Homes?"

"Yes," he answered through clenched teeth.

"Mr. Homes has been a manager. I am one of the owners. Your loyalty is with me." Anger flooded her cheeks. She leaned over the desk and threw her gloves on the ledger.

"Mrs. Homes. . .Nettie. I made a promise. . .to your father."

"My father?" she gasped and sat on the chair. The old schoolhouse clock ticked loudly, making the only sound between them. The old wall clock had been her one concession to him in remodeling the office.

Tice ran his hand across his chin and closed his eyes. Utter exhaustion mingled with a spark of relief in his eyes when he stared at her again. "The promise was made twenty-five years ago." He wrenched himself from his swivel chair and rummaged through the small safe behind his desk. "Here are the receipts. If you check them you will see everything I am about to tell you is true."

She stared at a packet of yellowed receipts that he threw on top of her gloves. "Tell me about them," she pleaded.

"A long time ago your father decided to make a yearly contribution, anonymously, to Schiffley churches. He didn't care about the denomination, only for the donor to always remain out of the public eye. Each year he selected a different church, alternating among the four. Now there are six and I do the same. The donation never became a part of the entry. That is the reason for the difference one month out of each year. Up until the time Mr. Homes took over there was never anyone to question it. He saw no reason to change the practice."

"But my father never professed to any religious influence." She remembered back to his deathbed wish to accept the Lord. Her breath came in short quivering gasps.

"Whatever his reasons, he never divulged them to me. Your father was a very private man."

"Derry knew but he was sworn to secrecy. He kept the tradition," she spoke half aloud. "Now that I know, I must confide in Elise."

"Of course." He rose and took his coat and hat from a

brass rack on the wall. With almost a dramatic flair, he removed a set of keys from his pocket and laid them on the desk. "I won't be needing these anymore. Mr. Homes will soon be back and you can work out some arrangement about the continuation of the mill," he said quietly.

Nettie stared up at him. "Whatever do you mean?"

"I have done my job. I have kept the confidence."

"But you showed me the paper from the safe where my father gave you permission to stay as long as you wanted."

"There is no paper, Nettie. I never actually let you read it, did I? I was bluffing. You know very well how to bluff. I'm surprised you didn't recognize the tactics." New lines creased his somber face. His large hands toyed with his hat. In spite of the solemnity of the occasion, he laughed aloud.

"You didn't have to tell me that, Mr. Tice," Nettie said in a voice filled with emotion. "I respect your loyalty to my father. Also, the loyalty you show to my family. I need your help. Please, stay." She held her hand across the desk, looking up at him with love and gratitude. "My father did you a great injustice by not giving you a guarantee of a lifetime position. I wonder if he ever realized what a dedicated worker he hired? My sister and I will appreciate your service for as long as you want to give it."

He held on to the back of the chair where he had directed the operations for countless years. After a long thoughtful moment he reached out and took her hand. He was unsmiling as he shook it vigorously. He harumphed loudly, quickly attending to a disorderly pile of papers on the corner of the desk. Then his fingers lingered by the set of keys. At last he picked them up and held them up to her. "I'll lock up after you are out of the building. By the way, don't think for a minute you can bully me into consenting for a pay raise for your 'darlings.' They make too much money as it is."

Nettie smiled as she drove home. Henry Tice had made her

want to laugh and cry. He definitely came from the old school. Her father would have been proud of him for his years of devoted service. Only the thought of her reunion with Derry furrowed her brow with lines of worry.

᪥

Derrick left Russ standing at the bottom of the staircase in the Traum after a hasty introduction to Mary. She ushered Russ into the parlor as Derrick hurried up the stairs to find Nettie. He flushed with frustration over the leg that refused to be hurried. Then, for all his haste, he stood outside the bedroom door for a long time before he turned the knob.

Nettie sat in the rocker, facing the window. She turned her head slightly, recognizing that someone stood behind her. "Mary?" Her hair flowed like golden fleece over her housecoat. The aroma of her perfume scented the room. "Mary?" she called again.

Derrick walked slowly around to stand before her. He heard a murmur of surprise escape her lips. Then he saw the child in her arms. He leaned over and kissed them both. "What a beautiful picture. I've often tried to conjure it in my mind but I never dreamed of such perfection."

Tears brimmed in her eyes and spilled down over her cheeks. "How often I dreamed of this moment. Oh, Derry." The baby looked curiously at the newcomer, then returned to his feeding.

"My son, my son. How I longed to see your sweet face." He took the child's small hand in his own and placed a hand on his head. "Does he know his name? Billy," he called softly.

"Derry, I have something to tell you." Nettie sat unmoving but her eyes clouded as she looked searchingly up at him.

"Words can wait, darling Nettie. It seems I have waited a lifetime to hold you in my arms." He circled the top of her shoulders with his arms and lay his head on hers as she sat there crying quietly. For a long time he stood there as the child stopped nursing and fell asleep.

"I long to hold you again, dearest." She wrapped the baby in a blanket and prepared to put him in his bed. "Wait until I lay him down," she whispered. Nettie carried the sleeping baby to his crib in the dressing room nearby. When she came back she took Derrick in her arms where he waited on the edge of the bed. His kisses covered her face, then hungrily, her lips. She tasted the salty tears from them both. She held him tightly, marveling at the instant recall she felt with his arms about her, the smell of his maleness, the feel of his cheek on hers. Then she took his hand and led him to the chaise at the far end of their room where they could talk more quietly. When he opened his mouth to speak, she held slender fingers across his lips. They sat, arm in arm, barely breathing in their bliss.

"I have something to tell you, my love. Don't speak or I will be unable to finish. Please, don't hate me, Derry. I couldn't bear it. Every day I berate myself because I haven't told you the whole truth. I ask God's mercy for being deceitful."

He took her hands in his and looked deeply into her sparkling, blue eyes. "Nettie, dearest. I could never hate you. We have so much to be thankful for today. Being apart from you has made me realize many things, but the most important is that I couldn't live on without you. You are my whole life, my reason for living."

She heard his promise and wanted to believe it with her whole heart. The dark eyes gazing back at her from his gaunt face pained her more than his words. She recognized his suffering and despair. She wanted to take him in her arms and comfort him, to erase the pain, the miles between them. But first she needed to unburden herself so that there was nothing but truth in their lives.

"I lied to you," she broke into wracking sobs. Nettie wrapped her arms about herself and kept him at a distance with those pain-filled eyes demanding to know her sin.

"Nettie, my darling, whatever it is I can forgive it. In the past I did many dreadful things that I ask you to forgive, as well.Let's begin with a clean slate with no bitterness between us. Whatever you think you have done it can't be worse then what I did when I left you so abruptly without telling you I was drafted. Can you ever forgive me for being such a coward?" He sobbed openly, holding his head in his hands. At last he searched her eyes. "Nothing in this world can be as horrible as the time we spent apart. I vow to you, from this day forward, there will be nothing but truth from my lips." He reached out and kissed her hand.

She dropped to her knees in front of him. Her head bowed. "You don't know, Derry. You don't know. Forgive me," she wept.

Silence and fear filled the room. Softly, with trembling hand he caressed her hair. Calm returned to her as he stroked the golden mass. "My poor darling. What you have been through without me."

"First I must tell you about Billy's name." She steeled herself to be calm, to speak the truth. "When you left I was. . . crushed. The only thing keeping me strong was the determination I learned from Papa. When I wanted to falter, his memory kept me going. When I wanted to quit and give up any hope of having a living child, I remembered how he worked and started with nothing and forged a company with bits and pieces. He was a determined man, Derry. I drew my strength from him. . .not from you. I'm sorry." She ran her fingers through his hair as he sat listening. "It seemed only logical for me to name the baby after him. Without Papa's memory, Billy wouldn't have been born."

"I understand, Nettie. I've given it much thought. At first I blamed you for not giving him my name but then I realized you needed something to hold on to. I don't blame you. I'm proud to know Billy is named after your father." He lifted her chin and kissed her soft lips, lingering over what seemed to be a memory. "If this is all you worried about, then there is nothing more to say."

She drew away from him and closed her eyes. She spoke so softly, so haltingly, he strained to hear. "Our son came into the world prematurely, after I had spent months in bed. He was so tiny he was placed in a little dresser drawer and kept by the warm oven. We didn't know if he would live. When Lise brought Jamie to me because he couldn't survive, I didn't even want to see him."

"Jamie?" he asked in a voice husky with fear. Derrick leaned back slightly, reeling from the implication of her confession. No longer did he interrupt. His heart hammered in his chest.

"But when I heard him cry that night I could not deny him Billy's place at my breast. He needed me and I needed him. Don't you see, God sent him to me. . .to us?"

"I don't understand. What are you telling me?" Stark fear showed in his eyes.

"I took him as my son, Derry. I held him and loved him. In a sense I became his mother. When Lise came to take him home to the orphanage, I refused to let her. In my heart he is our son." She stopped crying and a look of dread came over her face. "Please, say you will be a father to him."

Derrick stood up and walked away from her. He stared out of the window into the night. His heart ached by the weight of what she had told him. When she reached out to him, he stepped back as though mortally wounded. He ignored her extended hand.

With great determination she grasped his arm though it hung reluctantly at his side. Nettie's face no longer held sadness. It brimmed with relief. A new light shone in her eyes that came with unburdening her heart. "Come, I have told you the lie, now I want to show you the truth."

He followed slowly, as a prisoner being dragged reluctantly to his cell. Nettie led him out of their room and down the hall. She opened the door to a nursery with soft light glowing near a crib where a baby with silken yellow hair slept, oblivious to the world around him. There she waited until the look in Derrick's eyes registered one of complete surprise. "I want you to meet Billy, our son."

For a moment, Derrick blinked in confusion. When he comprehended the meaning of her words, great agony lifted from his chest. He leaned over the crib and made strange sobbing noises. When he lifted his eyes to Nettie, they overflowed with love. He sensed a new peace in her and he felt it in himself. He reached out and took her in his arms and held her as he had only dreamed in the past year. Derrick knew they had made it through the winds that blew in conflict. He was home again and this time with two little boys to call his sons.

❧

Alone in the parlor, Mary stared up into the dark eyes of Russell Parks. He stood awkwardly, waiting as she ushered him to the settee. She sat on the distant end.

"This room is just like I pictured it," Russ groped for conversation. "Derrick spoke about it many times."

"It's a beautiful house. I shall miss it." She found herself blushing.

He leaned forward. "Are you going somewhere?"

She laughed lightly. Her heart sang with uncommon joy. "I must return to Elise now that Mr. Homes is back. First I missed the children from the Haven when I came here. Now I will miss Nettie and the babies. Up until now I thought I had only one home."

"So much has happened. I thank you for your letters."

She nodded. "Some tea would be nice." She excused herself

and ran to the kitchen. When she returned, Russ was smiling, more relaxed than when she had first met him. He had moved a small table close to the settee where the tea tray was quickly deposited. Mary let out a sigh and sat closer to him. "I've been looking forward to meeting you." She poured tea and passed a plate of small sandwiches. As the hours slipped away into the night, they fell into a familiarity that was but an extension of their letters.

ॐ

The four of them stood watching the razing of the turrets, a project Nettie had initiated for Derrick's homecoming. She looked up at him, feeling his strength, sensing his new command of himself. "Our sons will be of the new world and not of the old. I thought you wouldn't mind if the turrets came down," she giggled.

"While I was away, I guess I thought about making some changes, too," he admitted. "I'm so glad you started this. One of the changes I wanted to make was to go back to work with my father, if he'll have me."

"I heard Papa say many times, 'When Derrick comes home he must come to work at the railroad again. I believe you could do anything you want, my hero."

For a moment he stared at her disapprovingly. "Don't ever say that, Nettie. The only heroes are the men buried in France." There was a catch in his voice. Russ came to stand beside him and he put a firm hand on Derrick's shoulder.

"He's right, you know, Nettie. Though Derrick did some pretty remarkable feats over there, the only heroes are those who made the supreme sacrifice. We will never forget them, nor should we."

Nettie and Mary waited until the men inspected the construction site where a new wing was being added to replace the turreted rooms. "What are your plans for going back to the Haven?" They walked arm in arm through the dormant garden.

"Of course, I'll go. Derrick is home again and you no longer need my—"

"Friendship," finished Nettie. "I will always need your friendship, Mary. Please stay a while, though. At least until I make arrangements for some help. I knew you would be leaving, so I made tentative plans with a young woman from the mill. I like her very much, but not as much as you," she hurried to add. "We didn't discuss it too much but I think Derry will let me manage the mill, with Mr. Tice's help, of course."

"Could you really work with that man?"

Nettie smiled and nodded. "I think we finally understand each other. My father must have seen something good in him years ago. And believe me, Willhelm Waller was not a man to give his trust easily. I think Mr. Tice and I are learning to respect each other." She turned on the path and looked back at the house where Derrick and Russ examined the new rafters that were recently put in place. "Tell me the truth, Mary. You don't really expect to return to the Haven, do you?"

Mary blushed and her gaze flew to Russ. "I don't think so. Chaplain Parks. . .is anxious to return to his church, though he feels they may give him a new assignment because of his absence. He has asked me to join him, as his wife, of course." Mary cried as Nettie embraced her. "Oh, now I will miss both you and Elise."

A short distance away, Derrick pumped Russ's hand. When Nettie and Mary walked back to their men, Derrick put his arm around Nettie and gazed lovingly into her soft, blue eyes.

"We are so fortunate," he declared as though he was toasting the four of them. "In the past year we have made lasting friendships, Nettie and I have found God and each other again, and we have not one, but two sons." He bent down and kissed his bride with a passion long absent from their lives. The four of them joined hands in a circle of love and understanding.

A Letter To Our Readers

Dear Reader:

In order that we might better contribute to your reading enjoyment, we would appreciate your taking a few minutes to respond to the following questions. When completed, please return to the following:

Rebecca Germany, Managing Editor
Heartsong Presents
P.O. Box 719
Uhrichsville, Ohio 44683

1. Did you enjoy reading *Crosswinds*?
   ❑ Very much. I would like to see more books
      by this author!
   ❑ Moderately
      I would have enjoyed it more if _____

   _____

2. Are you a member of **Heartsong Presents**? ❑Yes ❑No
   If no, where did you purchase this book?_____

   _____

3. What influenced your decision to purchase this
   book? (Check those that apply.)

   ❑ Cover   ❑ Back cover copy

   ❑ Title   ❑ Friends

   ❑ Publicity   ❑ Other_____

4. How would you rate, on a scale from 1 (poor) to 5
   (superior), the cover design?_____

5. On a scale from 1 (poor) to 10 (superior), please rate the following elements.

    __Heroine   __Plot

    __Hero   __Inspirational theme

    __Setting   __Secondary characters

6. What settings would you like to see covered in **Heartsong Presents** books?_____

_____

_____

7. What are some inspirational themes you would like to see treated in future books?_____

_____

_____

8. Would you be interested in reading other **Heartsong Presents** titles? ❑ Yes ❑ No

9. Please check your age range:
   - ❑ Under 18
   - ❑ 18-24
   - ❑ 25-34
   - ❑ 35-45
   - ❑ 46-55
   - ❑ Over 55

10. How many hours per week do you read? _____

Name _____

Occupation _____

Address _____

City_____ State_____ Zip _____

101
Ways to Say
"*I Love You*"

How do you say I love you? By sending love notes via overnight delivery. . .by watching the sunrise together. . . by calling in "well" and spending the day together. . .by sharing a candlelight dinner on the beach. . .by praying for the man or woman God has chosen just for you.

When you've found *the one*, you can't do without *one hundred and one ways* to tell them exactly how you feel. Priced to be the perfect subsitute for a birthday card or love note, this book fits neatly into a regular envelope. Buy a bunch and start giving today!

Specially Priced!
Buy 10 for only $9.97!
or 5 for only $4.97!

48 pages, Paperbound, 3½" x 5½"

·····Heart♥ong·····

HISTORICAL ROMANCE IS CHEAPER BY THE DOZEN!

Any 12 *Heartsong Presents* titles for only $26.95 **

Buy any assortment of twelve *Heartsong Presents* titles and save 25% off of the already discounted price of $2.95 each!

**plus $1.00 shipping and handling per order and sales tax where applicable.

HEARTSONG PRESENTS TITLES AVAILABLE NOW:

(If ordering from this page, please remember to include it with the order form.)

·········Presents·········

Great Inspirational Romance at a Great Price!

Heartsong Presents books are inspirational romances in contemporary and historical settings, designed to give you an enjoyable, spirit-lifting reading experience. You can choose wonderfully written titles from some of today's best authors like Peggy Darty, Tracie J. Peterson, Colleen L. Reece, Lauraine Snelling, and many others.

When ordering quantities less than twelve, above titles are $2.95 each.

Heart♥ng Presents
Love Stories Are Rated G!

That's for godly, gratifying, and of course, great! If you love a thrilling love story, but don't appreciate the sordidness of some popular paperback romances, **Heartsong Presents** is for you. In fact, **Heartsong Presents** is the *only inspirational romance book club*, the only one featuring love stories where Christian faith is the primary ingredient in a marriage relationship.

Sign up today to receive your first set of four, never before published Christian romances. Send no money now; you will receive a bill with the first shipment. You may cancel at any time without obligation, and if you aren't completely satisfied with any selection, you may return the books for an immediate refund!

Imagine. . .four new romances every four weeks—two historical, two contemporary—with men and women like you who long to meet the one God has chosen as the love of their lives. . .all for the low price of $9.97 postpaid.

To join, simply complete the coupon below and mail to the address provided. **Heartsong Presents** romances are rated G for another reason: They'll arrive *Godspeed!*